About the Author

Magenta is the pen name of a dreamer. One who enjoys all the smutty deliciousness romance can bring. One who knows how much real life can bring you down and knows the value of being able to escape into a pretend world. Pretend worlds where there is always a happy ever after.

Also by Magenta

<u>Arbor Vitae Coven</u>

(Paranormal Romance Series)

Candy Conniptions

Dreamy Delights

Fangs and Fireworks

(Coming 2023)

Christmas Capers

(Coming 2023)

Candy Conniptions

ARBOR VITAE COVEN
BOOK ONE

MAJENTA

Candy Conniptions
Arbor Vitae Coven 1

Mobi format: : 978-0-6453753-7-4
Print: : 978-0-6453753-7-4

Cover design by Dazed Designs
Edited by Elemental Editing

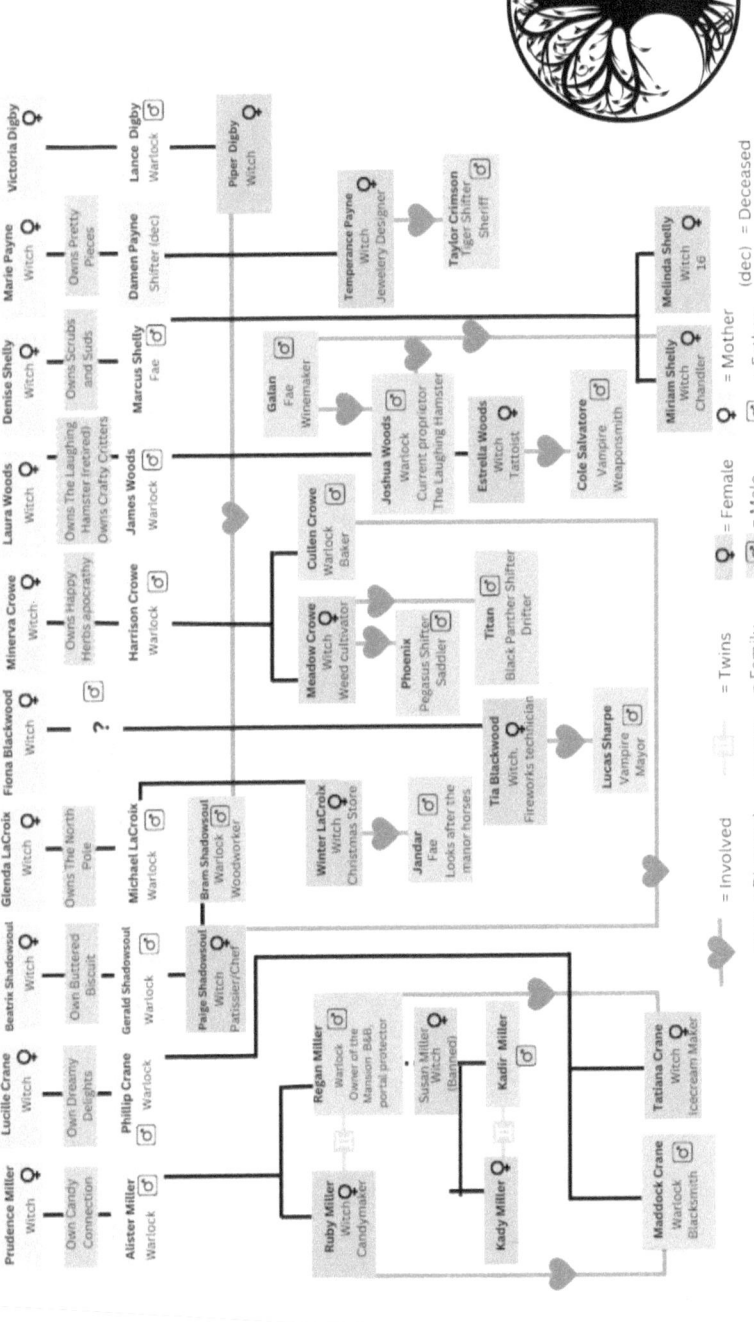

Prologue

"This meeting of the Matrons of Morbank Island may come to order," Prudence Miller announces as she bangs her gavel on the podium in front of her. She peers out at the rest of the ladies in the large room of the town hall. "Come now, settle down." The noise of the room slowly quiets, and the other nine women look up with curiosity.

"Prudence, what's this meeting about?" Victoria Digby questions. "You know I love meeting with you ladies, but usually drinks and nibbles are involved."

"Town affairs *are* better solved with a mojito in hand," Glenda La Croix adds with a laugh and a wave of her hand. A tittering of giggles explodes from the ladies, but when they see that Prudence is not laughing and wears a very somber look on her face, they all quiet down quickly.

"Ladies, I think we all know why we are meeting here. The portal is fading, and there isn't enough power generation to hold it open anymore. We are failing the realms. Action needs to be taken. If not, the council will appoint another coven to Morbank, and we'll get kicked off our ancestral island," Prudence says with an expression of sadness on her face. "It's time for the next generation to step up and take their rightful place at the head of the family businesses. We're all ready to retire, and the creative ideas just aren't flowing like they used to." The women all nod their heads in agreement, and Prudence continues with a hitch in her voice. "There's also something else that I have to tell you."

"Oh, Prudence dear, what's wrong?" Lucille Crane asks as she gets up and puts her arm around Prudence. "What's making you so sad?"

"Don't you think it's strange that all of our oldest daughters have left town, even though every single one of them is in the family business?" she asks, looking at the ladies. The ladies start talking amongst themselves.

"I did think it was strange that they all decided to leave town and learn from other artists, but they are young and independent," Laura Woods exclaims, shrugging.

"Yes," Fiona Blackwood adds, staring down at her hands. "I understand why Tia went to China, but I always thought she'd come back when she finished learning what she wanted. Instead, she stays." Fiona's face is covered in sadness. "I keep trying to get her to come home, but she avoids the topic."

"I have similar conversations with Tatiana," Lucille inserts. "She's so busy with that boyfriend of hers." The sneer on her face when she says this makes it obvious she isn't too keen on him.

"Ladies, ladies," Prudence says, hugging Lucille and encouraging her to sit back down. She straightens her shoulders and takes a big breath. "When that slut Susan ran off and left Regan," she starts, looking very sad.

"May she suffer pox on her pussy," the other nine ladies murmur in unison, one of them spitting to the side.

A small smile appears on Prudence's face. "Amen, my loyal ladies. When that happened, and Ruby didn't come home to help her brother and his babies, I knew there was something very wrong. Not only that, but when I hired someone else to run the shop, she didn't even bat an eye. Once upon a time, that would have made her come home on a warpath. Nobody was allowed to run her shop except her, so I conducted some research. What I discovered may surprise you."

The women look on eagerly, waiting for her to continue.

"Well, don't make us wait. What have you found out?" Laura questions.

"The girls are under a powerful repulsion spell," she announces. Gasps and shocked chatter erupt, but she talks over them, and they calm down to listen. "The signs were all there, we just didn't acknowledge them. One, they all suddenly left town around the same time. Two, none have shown any interest in coming home. I know for certain it was Ruby's dream to take over the candy store. For her to up and leave all of a sudden was suspicious. She's been gone for eighteen months now and has shown no interest in coming home," she says, wringing her hands together.

"I think part of the dwindling power problem is that we are all getting older and the businesses need a new influx of power. With the lack of new, creative inspiration, the tourists have lost interest. All of us are looking to retire, and if the girls don't come home and take over, we will have to sell the businesses or close them down. An artisan village with no artisans has no draw. So, with my suspicions, I cast a detection spell. I have discovered that this town, and our places of business and homes in particular, have a repelling spell on them specifically aimed at the girls."

More gasps and outrageous cries fill the hall.

"Who could have done such a thing and why?" Marie Payne questions. A shadow of sadness haunts her eyes, her skin is sallow, and she looks like she has lost weight. Pru makes a note to visit her soon.

"Well, that's the all-important question, isn't it?" Prudence says with a glare in her gray eyes and steel in her voice. "I will be informing Sheriff Crimson of my findings, but that is not going to solve our problem."

"I see by the look on your face that you have a plan," Victoria remarks with a smile. "Don't be coy, share."

"You bet your ass I have a plan," Prudence retorts with a determined look on her face. "I have found a spell to counteract it, but there may be some negative side effects. I need all of you ladies to think about this quite carefully, because once it's done, there's no going back. The negative impacts could affect you directly."

"I don't know about everyone else, but if someone is messing with my girl and that's why she won't come home to visit her mama, then I'm in!" Beatrix Shadowsoul shouts, getting to her feet.

"That's right," Marie agrees, also getting to her feet. "Nobody messes with our kids or town and gets away with it."

By this time, all the ladies are on their feet and agreeing to the spell. A tear appears in the corner of Prudence's eye. She smiles and looks around at the other women in the room.

"My sisters, I knew I could count on you, just as we have been counting on each other since we first formed this coven so many years ago."

"That's right, witches for life," Denise shouts.

"Or bitches, as the case may be, hey, Denise," Lucille teases cheekily, bumping her hip against Denise's.

"Well, you would know," Denise replies with a grin.

"Okay, ladies, settle down. We will meet in the clearing behind the manor at midnight tomorrow night. It is a full moon and the best time to fulfill the spell. Please bring something from your girls with you to use in the spell. It must be something that means a lot to them," Prudence announces with a satisfied smile. "I don't know who did this, but the backlash when we break the spell will let them know we are onto them. We must prepare to ward off a takeover."

"We will have to be more vigilant. We have grown complacent. Although we know most of the people in town, there are always people coming and going," Minerva Crowe muses out loud. "Someone is trying to start trouble, maybe a coven from another town."

"Let's keep this to ourselves for now or at least until I can speak to Sheriff Crimson. Now go, and don't forget to perform your purification rituals. I will see you all tomorrow night." Prudence shoos the ladies away.

The ladies all make their way out of the hall and return to their businesses or their daily routines.

Prudence collapses in a chair and rubs her head to ward off the pounding pressure behind her eyes. The counter spell could have some far-flung and dire consequences, but it's needed to break such a strong curse. Saying that, however, there isn't much these ladies wouldn't do for their oldest daughters. Picking up her handbag, she places it over her shoulder, straightens her shirt, and smooths down her skirt before reaching to do the same with her hair. Then, with a deep breath and her head held high, she strides out of the hall toward the sheriff's office to have a quiet, confidential conversation with Sheriff Crimson.

The moon is high and round in the sky, and the night has a bite of cold to it with that sharp smell of the coming fall. The trees are losing their leaves, and the leaf litter is scattered all over the ground of the clearing. Back through the trees, a single light can be seen in the manor, left on for late-night visitors and portal users.

The Manor Bed and Breakfast is the location of the supernatural portal, which links all the realms to Earth for the US region. Every kind of creature passes through, but even then, it doesn't mean you won't find humans staying there, since the supernatural world is a new curiosity.

One by one, the ladies drift out from the trees, coming from different directions. All ten of them are wearing their scarlet red coven robes with gold thread woven throughout in intricate designs. Hoods are pulled up to cover their heads, and their hands clasp lit white candles. As they make a circle in the clearing, Prudence reaches under her robe and pulls a satchel off her shoulder, and the other ladies follow suit.

Reaching into the bag, she pulls out an athame and her spell book, which she places next to her, and then she walks to the center of the clearing. There is a fire pit with a cauldron, filled with salt and water, sitting over the top. With one word and gesture from Pru, the fire bursts to life and starts crackling, the blue and red flames casting an eerie light around the clearing. The ladies blow out their candles and place them into their bags before setting them to the side, while Prudence grabs the athame and moves back to the cauldron.

"Please bring the object precious to your daughter forward and place it into the cauldron. We will need a few drops of your blood as well. Then let us join hands for the incantation."

Each lady places the object into the cauldron. Using the athame, they drip a couple of drops of their blood into the water, and the steam drifting off the top takes on a red hue. With this task complete, they step back and join hands. Prudence adds a handful of bay and sage leaves to the water and moves to join the others, starting the chant.

"Oh Hecate, hear us now, I call upon thee to hear our pleas. Come forth and cleanse our first-born daughters of all evil and alien magics intending harm and restore them to balance, health, and home. We thank you, and by our wills combined, so mote it be."

"So mote it be," the coven repeats.

With a loud boom, a flash of purple bursts outwards from the cauldron, flowing through all the women in the circle and continuing outward. When the light dissipates, the fire dies, and the spell is complete.

"Now all we can do is wait," Prudence announces.

"Well, I don't know about anyone else, but that was thirsty work. Who's up for a drink?" Marie asks as she walks back to her bag. Pulling out a couple of bottles of wine, she hands them out before opening one and taking a swig.

Once the tense atmosphere breaks, the ladies laugh. They all take seats around the cauldron and more bottles of wine appear, as do a couple of joints. Smoke drifts on the breeze, pungent and pervasive. They talk quite loudly and joyously when a rustle in the trees causes them to drop into silence.

"What was that?" Lucille asks.

Victoria jumps up, grabbing the athame from the cauldron and brandishing it in front of herself. "I don't know, but they are going to have to go through me to get to you!" she says ferociously.

The ladies all look at each other and burst into laughter. Regan, Prudence's son, walks out of the trees. He's the man who lives in and runs the Manor Bed and Breakfast and polices the beings that come and go.

He has a wry look on his face as he addresses the coven. "Evening, ladies, Mother." He nods his head at them. "I could hear you from inside and felt the pressure wave from the spell." He raises an eyebrow at Victoria. "Did you forget you could use magic to defend yourself?" He laughs, gesturing to the athame.

She blushes and puts the athame back before retaking her seat as he continues.

"That's what you get for addling your brains with wine and herbs. Aren't you all a little old for partying hard?" He chuckles as they squirm like teenagers who have been caught by their parents. Looking around, he observes, "I notice there are no men from the coven at this little ceremony. You certainly didn't send me an invite."

Pru sputters at the comment. "This spell needed pure maternal energy."

He raises his eyebrow skeptically. "Did it, Mom? Or did you ladies want to have a little full moon party without the old ball and chains? Keys are to go into the bowl." He gestures to them, holding out a fruit bowl. "Your loved ones will thank me in the morning. Beds are made up for you in the manor. Try not to wake my children or the few guests I do have when you come in. Also, make sure you magic those rooms clean in the morning, I don't have enough staff at the moment to be picking up after grown-ass women."

The ladies sheepishly pull their keys out and drop them in the bowl.

He walks back toward the manor. "Have a good evening, ladies. I really hope the spell worked."

"So do we, Regan, so do we," his mother says as he walks away.

CHAPTER
One

Ruby

The bitter smell of burnt fudge wafts its way through the store as I slowly follow my new boss. He's prattling on about the changes he's making to the shop. Great, that pan can go in the trash now that the batch I was making has gone up in smoke. Even soaking it won't remove the burnt sugar from the bottom. The asshole wouldn't wait for me to finish the new recipe I was trying out.

His hands fly around as he articulates, but all I hear is *blah, blah, blah*. Mr. Whitmore Jr is nothing like his father. His father was a great, old-fashioned man who had a particular set of morals and standards. He was always impeccably dressed, and his gray hair, beard, and round-lensed glasses gave him a Santa Claus quality that everyone just adored—not to mention his natural jolly disposition and the sweet samples he was always handing out.

No, Junior is a very pale imitation of a Whitmore. Junior is the epitome of greedy man syndrome. He is wearing a cheap, ill-fitted polyester suit and a pinched look on his face. Where Senior had a jolly, round Santa body, Junior is just fat with great big jowls that wobble when he talks and huge sweat stains around his armpits. The stench wafting off him is unhygienic and unappealing. He has also completely abandoned samples and interacting with customers.

It seems like the bottom line is the only thing of importance to him. The way he sees it, the store will become like any other chain store. He believes efficiency and non-personalized service is the way of the future, not things such as tradition and family.

"And from now on, we won't be making any of that damn candy in store. It's more economical to buy in bulk from suppliers," the asshole chatters in front of me. My ears tune back in and prick up as he says this.

"I'm sorry, did you just say we wouldn't be making candy anymore, Mr. Whitmore?" I query with a frown on my face. He turns to me with an exasperated look.

"Yes, Ruby, that's exactly what I said. We'll be

tearing down the candy kitchen and placing more shelving space for packaged candy. We'll stock it with old standards like Peeps, Twinkies, and candy corn, to name a few."

My mouth drops open in astonishment. "But, but… that's what makes our store so popular. People come from miles around to watch the candy being made and then end up spending money. What will encourage people to visit us if we are the same as any other candy store? Plus, Mr. Whitmore Sr assured me I'd always have a position here at this store," I argue.

A knowing grin spreads over his face. "Well yes, Dad was always a dreamer, but in this economy, we just can't afford to pay you the wage he was paying you. You still have a job, but I'm afraid you'll just be a salesgirl from now on, not a 'candy artisan,'" he says, putting his fingers up in quotation marks, the sarcastic bastard.

My stomach drops, and tears fill my eyes. Mr. Whitmore Sr has only been gone a week. He died of a sudden unexpected heart attack, and nothing could be done. His funeral was just yesterday. How can a man be so heartless? How can he be making so many drastic changes? I straighten my spine. "I was under the impression that Mr. Whitmore Sr stipulated in his will there were to be no changes to the store. He said he had made arrangements for my job security."

At this, his sly grin grows wider. "Ah yes, Ruby, but there's a caveat. If the store is in financial trouble, changes are allowed, and since the store is now in dire financial straits, I can do what I want with it."

"Dire financial straits?" I question. "But business is booming. My fudge line popularity is at an all-time high, and I'm always being asked to make new flavors. The new image candy is flying off the shelves, not to mention the future wedding orders I have. The taffy line is also highly requested. I was thinking about employing someone to help. Inquiries on the Facebook page and email are skyrocketing with referrals and word of mouth. We couldn't be in better shape."

"Cancel them," he demands. "It's too much work. We just don't have time, nor will I be hiring someone to help." He waddles off toward the back rooms.

I stand still, absolutely stunned. Did he just tell me to cancel the orders? What the fuck? It will kill the store. I look sadly around the shop. The clean white lines of the candy kitchen sparkle despite the smoke still lingering in the air from the burnt batch of fudge. The display area is a riot of color, exhibiting all the taffy and image candy, the display cabinet has blocks of fudge appealingly presented, waiting for people to order and be cut to size, and jars of colorful candy line the walls.

Mr. Whitmore Sr took all my prior knowledge and channeled it into different avenues of creativity. He sent me to master confectioners to learn various techniques and installed the kitchen for me to drum up more interest. Showing our clients how their candy was made, as well as free tastings, were ways of expanding people's tastes. Then, hopefully, they would buy more. He was a tremendous mentor to me. Without him, the thought of being here just isn't the same. It isn't home anymore.

With the thought of home, a burst of incredible energy floats through my body like a current of electricity racing through my limbs. A shiver runs down my back, my hair stands on end, and goosebumps break out over my skin. All of a sudden, everything is so much clearer. Smells are stronger, sounds are crisper, and my mind feels like it's operating on all cylinders again. It's like I was in a fog, and now everything is sharp and focused. I shake my head.

Home! What was I thinking? This isn't home, nor has it ever been. It's a temporary stop on my journey. Home is the Candy Connection back at Morbank, and my family—I haven't seen my family for over eighteen months. I could go stay with my brother. I've been such a bad aunty and sister recently. My poor motherless niece and nephew could probably do with some female influence, one that wasn't their grandma anyway. I really don't know why I hadn't thought about this before.

I don't have many close friends here, except for Mr. Whitmore. All the girls that I consider sisters are scattered throughout the country and the world. I have no boyfriend to speak of, only a few one-night stands here or there, and certainly no one I'd bring home to my mother.

Reality just jumped up and smacked me in the face. This isn't where I belong. I'm going home. Frowning, I wonder why it's taken me so long to realize this. I can't actually remember having any conversations with my parents, brother, or girlfriends in a long time.

Decision made, I stalk back into the kitchen, gathering my recipes and designs. There is no way I'm leaving them behind to be trashed, or worse, sold. I also gather all of my own flavorings. I always bought small samples when trying new things, since there was no point in Mr. Whitmore buying industrial-sized flavors if they didn't sell. Shoving them all into the backpack I carry to work, I move out to the floor and grab some samples of all the things I made. I want to show my mom and dad some new ideas for the shop. Next, I slice a few pieces of the different flavored fudges I created and place them in a sample box. All of these get put into my backpack as well. Luckily it didn't have much in it other than my keys and phone.

The store phone starts ringing, and the bell above the door chimes as a few customers walk in. I ignore the phone and tell the customers someone will be with them in a minute.

I can hear Junior prattling on in the back room, so I take my backpack and move toward the sound. I find him talking to someone on the phone while perusing the inventory.

"Ah, excuse me, Mr. Whitmore?" I say.

He turns around and faces me, phone in hand. "What is it, Ruby?" he asks impatiently. "I'm on a call."

"You can take this job and shove it up your ass. I quit!" I announce, leaving him standing there with a shocked expression on his face and a voice shouting at him through the phone.

Turning, I walk out of the back door to the nearby metal staircase. It runs up to the second-story apartment above the store. Mr. Whitmore Sr allowed me to live there because I sometimes worked late into the night, filling orders or stocking up if we were running low. It isn't much, but it's rent free, and I could come and go to the store as needed.

My steel cap boots clatter against the steps as I run up the stairs. It came furnished, so I basically only have my personal items to pack. I open the door, throw my backpack onto the bench, and run to the closet next to the bed, pulling down two suitcases.

After tossing all my clothes into one of the cases, I then go to the bookshelf and grab the few novels I have, as well as my spell books which are glamoured to look like recipe books. Even though few people came up to my apartment, if they did, they never would have guessed I was a witch.

I haven't done many spells since leaving Morbank

Island. Every time I tried, they either failed or I lost interest. It's something to talk to my mom about when I see her—if she's not too angry at me. God, I am going to be in so much trouble. Family first is my mother's favorite catchphrase, and I haven't been living by that motto.

All the books go in with my clothes, along with the homemade quilt on the end of my bed and the few pieces of jewelry I own, which were made by one of my friends. Zipping it closed, I start on the other case. I fill it with my shoes, personal items from the bathroom, and a few other witch items like my mortar and pestle. After closing the second suitcase, I run downstairs to my old, beat-up Mustang convertible and throw my bags into the trunk.

Hurrying back upstairs, I empty the litter tray into the trash, give it a rinse, and then dry it out. I reach into the overhead cabinets and pull out tins of cat food, the bag of dry food, and the portable water bottle I have and place them in the tray. Opening another cupboard, I pull out the cat carrier and look at the window seat. Sitting there is my seal point Ragdoll, Sugar. She never moves far from the window, because she likes to overlook her domain like a queen surveying her subjects.

"Come on, Sugar," I murmur, picking her up and rubbing my face against her lovely soft fur. "Let's blow this joint. It's time to go home where Kadir and Kady will give you all the loving you can take."

Placing her into the carrier, I close the door and sit down at the table, quickly opening my laptop. I shoot a group email to all of my future orders explaining the situation. I tell the ones who paid a deposit to contact Mr. Whitmore Jr personally and then attach his phone number. I also give everyone my personal details and phone number, and let them know I am relocating and will be able to fill orders again in two weeks. Fingers crossed I will be able to keep the majority of my clients.

Luckily, I have nothing on order for the next two weeks, so that will give me time to find somewhere to stay, set up, and talk to my mom and dad. Closing the laptop and shoving it in its bag, I throw it over my shoulder and look around to make sure I haven't missed anything. I pick up my backpack and phone off the bench, grab the cat carrier, and pull the door closed behind me before I jog back downstairs.

Mr. Whitmore comes jogging—well, jogging for a short little fat man—around the corner. "Ruby, where are you going? What am I going to do without a salesgirl?" he whines. "Who's going to run the store and talk to customers?" His face shrivels up at the thought.

"Well, Mr. Whitmore, I suggest you call one of the actual salesgirls in. I'm the candy maker, not the salesgirl," I tell him, placing my backpack and laptop on the passenger seat. Pulling the driver's seat forward, I put Sugar on the back seat before I turn to look at him.

"But, Ruby," he starts, and I put my hand up.

"No, Mr. Whitmore, just no. I'm done." I get in my car, cranking the engine. Music blasts out of the speakers, and with Queen singing about biting the dust, I tear out of the alleyway, throwing my hand out the window and flipping him the bird. A billow of smoke blasts from the exhaust, leaving a lasting impression.

I laugh as I watch his face in the rearview mirror. It screws up and turns red, and then he starts coughing and waving his hands around, trying to clear the exhaust. Karma is a bitch.

As I leave the city, it's like a weight has left my body. My mind is light and genuinely joyful for the first time in as long as I can remember. I'm on my way home. I don't know why I didn't do it sooner.

CHAPTER
Two

Ruby

T he return to my hometown took two days, with a few rest stops for both me and Sugar and an overnight stay in a seedy little roadside motel. It looked like it could have been on an episode of CSI, but it had a bed, and I was tired.

The trip was full of contemplation. Why had it taken me so long to return to my home? I was always very close with my family, and the town was a bustling hub of tourism, so it was never monotonous. There was no reason for me to stay away, but something always seemed to distract me or come up when I thought about returning.

Morbank Island is located in the Thousand

Islands between New York and Canada, on the Canadian side. It's also the location for the portal that connects this continent to the supernatural realms. It's an excellent place for it to be located because it's only accessible by boat. This makes it safer for the supes who live there and the ones who use the portal to travel between realms. It also makes it easier to regulate human tourists that come and go. Supes were outed to humans a few years ago, and although there were some bumpy patches, everything is mostly civilized these days. Humans are still curious, however, as supes tend to keep to themselves.

While we make the final leg of our journey, I watch the calm waters of the St. Lawrence River pass by as the ferry makes its way to the island. The wildlife is in abundance, with birds nesting on the banks and the occasional splash of water from hungry fish.

As one of the largest islands in the area, we support a substantial town with a thriving tourism industry. Morbank's architecture is based on quaint medieval design, and the manor, which my brother and I inherited from our grandparents when they decided to retire, is the premier accommodation spot for the town.

My brother is now in charge of the resort and staff, and as much as I love the place, I never wanted to be involved. I always wanted to run my parent's candy store. Hopefully they will forgive me and allow me to continue that dream.

My heart beats a million miles an hour as the ferry docks. Driving my car off the boat, I head toward town. Main Street is lined with oak trees, and wrought iron, old-fashioned lamp posts are situated between each one. Most are automatic, but a few around the town center get lit by a town lamplighter. The tourists get a real kick out of it.

Tourists aren't allowed to bring their cars into town. They must be parked at the dock in secure parking, and then they are transported around by horse and carriage—another thing they get a kick out of. Townies, however, are allowed to drive around.

Turning away from the main commercial district, I drive toward the resort. The entry is blocked by a large, wrought iron gate that's activated by driving over a strip. The entrance, at the moment, is closed, and I can see a well-built man working on it as I drive closer. An anti-flash mask is covering his face, and the welder in his hand sends sparks shooting into the air as he welds a piece of the gate. I slow the car to a stop, put on the hand brake, and get out, shielding my eyes as I walk toward the man.

He is leaning over, but I can see he's tall and has broad shoulders. He's covered head to toe in overalls, though, so I can't make out anything else. I wait patiently for the noise to finish and look up just as he lifts his face shield. He drops the welder handpiece and bends down to grab a bottle of water sitting next to him. The man opens the top and pours the liquid down his throat, and I can see the muscles in his neck working as he swallows. He then lifts the bottle and dumps the rest of the water over his head before turning to face me.

Holy shit. It's Maddock Crane, my brother's best friend and a former major crush of mine.

His dark tousled hair is plastered against his head. Trickles of water run down his chiseled jaw, which is covered in stubble, then drip off his chin. His dark eyes are cold, his lush lips are set in a straight line, and a wrinkle appears between his eyes and across his forehead as he looks at me.

"Well, well, well, look what the cat dragged in," he says with a sarcastic drawl. "Whatever could have happened to bring you back here, Miss Ruby, to live with the unsophisticated plebs?"

Damn, it seems like Maddock is pissed. This doesn't bode well for the reactions I'm going to get from my family. "Hey, Maddock." I wave sheepishly. "Long time no see. Is something wrong with the gate?" I inquire, ignoring the sarcasm spewing from him.

"Nope, just doing some repairs Regan asked for. Does he know you're coming? What about your parents?" he asks without warmth in his voice.

I stand here awkwardly, swinging my body back and forth before clasping my hands in front of me.

"Nope, spur-of-the-moment decision. Something made me realize I hadn't been home in a while, so I decided a trip home was needed."

A skeptical gleam flares in his eyes, and his eyebrows rise before he smooths out his face and says, "I'm sure they'll be happy to see you. Just give me a moment, and I'll get the gate open." He turns to clean up his gear, and my stomach drops at his cold, impersonal reaction. We used to be good friends, so I guess me staying away has damaged something else as well.

I get back into my car, muttering to Sugar, "The bastard's still as hot as ever. It's a pity he's as prickly as a cactus." She just continues to lick her butt. I laugh and watch as he moves his gear, unable to see much because his overalls make him look like a blob. Maybe he has a beer belly under there. He's good friends with Joshua Woods, and his family are the local beer brewers who run the tavern.

"What do you think, Sugar? Is there a beer gut under there?" She just ignores me, continuing her hard work. "Slow down, Sugar," I scold, wrinkling my nose. "You're going to sand that butthole down to nothing."

Maddock moves his gear to the side of the gate, where I can see a pickup truck behind the wall. I watch as he pops the buttons on his overalls and peels them down. His torso is naked underneath. Hot damn! His body is fine. His broad shoulders lead to a wide chest with bulging biceps and defined pectoral muscles that taper down to a very flat stomach.

"Why, Sugar?" I complain. "Why couldn't he be fat?" I check my rearview mirror to make sure no drool has escaped my mouth.

With a wave of his hand, his warlock powers activate the gate, and it starts to swing open. I put my car into drive, and with a nod to him, I drive up to the manor.

"No distractions," I tell Sugar. "Who needs a man when we have a BOB and candy?"

I'm not sure she believes me, but butt licking definitely takes priority over my personal drama.

Putting the Mustang into park in front of the manor, I look up at the old girl. She's been in our family as long as the portal and village have been on this island. The regal-looking stone building is covered in copious amounts of variegated green ivy, and its various wings cast afternoon shadows over the circular, cobbled driveway. The manor's towering, decorative spires and darkened windows lend an almost sinister appearance to an otherwise elegant building.

I take a deep breath and grab Sugar's carrier and my backpack, easing out of the Mustang. With a start, I realize a blond teenage boy is waiting for me to get out—one I don't recognize, which is unusual in this town. "Oh, sorry, I didn't see you there," I tell him breathlessly.

He puts his hand out and smiles patiently at me. "No worries. If you give me your keys, I'll park the car for you," he offers, holding out his hand.

"Valet service?" I ask, raising my eyebrows. "Since when do we have a valet service?" I wonder out loud.

"Well, ma'am, I've been working here for the last eight months," he says gently. I gape at him in stunned silence. He just smiles again and slides behind the wheel of my car, starts it, and drives it behind the building, smoke belching out as he goes around the corner. Hmm, I really need to get that looked at. Damn! My luggage! I'll have to grab it later.

Walking slowly up the steps, I rehearse what I'll say to my brother. The front door is silent on its hinges when I walk into the foyer, my Converse soundless across the polished wooden floors. A long, elegant reception desk sits directly in front of the entrance where it can't be missed. Off to the left of the desk is a classic, old-fashioned elevator that services all the floors. To the right is the graceful, sweeping staircase leading up to the second-floor balcony that overlooks the foyer. A stylish bar and cocktail area are located up there, as well as the dining room for the patrons. Next to the lift is a comfy seating space and the concierge desk containing pamphlets for all the artisan businesses in the area. Large, wide windows allow for plenty of light to flow in, and the smell of sandalwood permeates the air from the potpourri bowls discretely located around the foyer. Dotted around the lobby are paintings of the island and Miller ancestors, who look very dour and severe. After pausing to take it all in, I head to the reception desk.

A sleek blonde woman stands behind it, her head down as she types away at a monitor in front of her. "Name?" she asks rather rudely and with a bored tone as I approach the desk. Placing Sugar's carrier and my backpack on the ground, I wait for her to look up. She doesn't. Well, that really won't do. What kind of people is my brother employing? I am about to call her out on her attitude when I hear the clatter of feet and the chattering of children's voices coming down the main staircase.

The woman behind the desk pops her head up, and she wears a look of annoyance as she ignores me completely and hurries in the direction of the noise. Stopping abruptly, she points at the cat carrier. "No pets allowed."

Without even waiting for me to say anything, she disappears up the grand staircase and out of sight. Following behind her, I hear her scolding the ones responsible for the noise quite severely, her harsh voice carrying easily through the space.

"What are you doing? What is all this ridiculous

noise? We are a refined, elegant place, not a zoo. Stop the noise at once."

I follow her voice and find her holding the arms of two frightened-looking children tightly. The girl has her dark red hair in pigtails, freckles across her button nose, and tears sliding down her face from her pretty green eyes. The boy has a look of stubborn determination, his arms are crossed defensively over his body, and his freckled nose is wrinkled in defiance. He shakes his head at her in what looks to be an argument. I lean against the wall and do what I do best, interfere.

"Well, considering their father owns this place, and it is family friendly accommodation, I'm going to go out on a limb and say they aren't doing anything wrong."

The woman eyes me with derision. "Why don't you mind your own business?" she sneers.

My eyebrows climb into my hair with shock. "Excuse me, is that the way you treat paying customers?" I ask incredulously.

The children turn to face me, and their eyes light up with joy. They wrench themselves free from the woman's grip and run toward me, shouting, "Aunty Ruby!" They throw themselves into my arms so hard I'm dragged down to the ground where I'm smothered in kisses and hugs, listening to their happy chatter with a warmth I haven't felt in forever. It's like being able to breathe after being underwater for so long.

I hear a clattering of heels as the woman strides toward us, smoothing out her pencil skirt and putting her hair back into place. "This is your aunt?" she questions the children with an insincere smile on her face.

I set the children down and stand up, straightening myself out. "Yes, their aunt. Consider this your notice, you're fired."

She blinks at me and starts stuttering, "You... You can't do that."

"Actually, I can! I own half this business, and from what I just witnessed, you are not the type of person we want working in a family hotel. How did you get a job here anyway?" I look her up and down. "I've never seen you before, and you are not from this town. Who are you?"

"Screw you," she snaps at me. "You just fired me. I don't have to tell you anything."

She stomps toward the reception desk and snatches up a handbag. Placing it over her shoulder, she rushes toward the front door. I wave my finger in her direction, and one of the heels on her shoes breaks, causing her to stumble. She throws a furious look at me over her shoulder and grabs it off her foot, then she continues to limp toward the door, throw it open, and march through before slamming it behind her.

"Well, I guess that's that," I say, turning to the twins as I brush my hands together like they are dirty.

"Good widdance," Kadir says, his little face scrunched up. Hmm, sounds like someone's spent a lot of time with Grandma. I smile at him.

"She was so mean," Kady whispers, her little hand grabbing hold of mine tightly. "Are you here to stay, Aunt Ruby?"

"Yes, Aunty Wuby," Kadir says. "Please say you're staying, we have missed you so much."

"Oh, my babies," I coo as I bend down and scoop them into my arms for more hugs. "I have missed you so much too. Yes, I'm here to stay. Maybe not here at the manor, but I'm not leaving town again. Now, where's Daddy?" They start cheering and jumping up and down in excitement.

Just as I ask, I look up and find my brother standing at the top of the stairs looking slightly stunned. His red hair is tousled like he has been running his hands through it regularly, and he looks tired and drawn. "Ruby, is that you?" he questions, rubbing his eyes. "Holy shit, it worked."

He races down the stairs and sweeps me up into his arms, swinging me around. He also covers my face in kisses, just like his children did, the stubble on his face scratching mine. Tears of joy stream down my face as I try to push him away. He puts me down and holds me at arm's length.

"Wow, this is not the reaction I thought I would get, but I will definitely take it."

"Sis, we missed you so much. Whatever kept you away doesn't matter, you're back now." He starts to frown. "You are back now, yes?" he questions, and I pat the side of his face in reassurance.

"Yes, Regan, I'm back."

"Awesome!" he says as he takes my hand and drags me toward the now unmanned reception desk. "Julie," he calls out. "Julie! Where is she?" He leans over the desk. Maybe he thinks she is hiding underneath. I wince and look at the children, holding a finger up to my mouth in the universal signal for silence.

The children giggle behind their hands, and I just whistle casually. Regan turns to look at me. "What did you do?" he asks me with a growl. "Where is Julie?"

"Oh, was that her name?" I inquire innocently, and the children continue to giggle.

Regan looks at them. "What did she do?" I shake my head at them behind his back, but the little traitors cave under his stern scowl, throwing themselves at his legs.

"Daddy, she was so mean to us. We were just coming down the stairs and talking, and she gwabbed us and started yelling," Kadir whines.

"Yes!" Kady chimes in. "She hurt my arm. Look!"

She shows Regan the red marks on her arm, and he looks up at me in shock.

"I saw her manhandling the kids for no reason, not to mention how rude she was to me when I walked in, so I fired her. Sorry if I overstepped," I apologize to him.

He has a look of surprise on his face. "Oh, thank God!" He sighs in relief, slumping against the desk. "I have wanted a reason to fire her for a while now. She's very pushy, if you know what I mean," he says slyly while looking between the two children. My brother is a very handsome man, it's no wonder she was pushy. "Let me call in a new receptionist for the day, and then we will get you settled," he says while going behind the desk and picking up a phone. "Give me ten minutes."

CHAPTER
Three

Maddock

I watch as the faded, cherry red Mustang drives through the gate and up the driveway until I can no longer see it, the feelings in my chest confusing the cold logic in my head. My heart is beating with excitement at seeing Ruby again, but my brain reminds me that she abandoned us and left to seek fame and fortune elsewhere. She promised not to be gone long, but she broke that promise.

When Susan took off and left Regan all alone with two babies to raise, Regan was heartbroken. Having his sister there, his twin, would have gone a long way in soothing that broken heart. They were so close I thought for sure Ruby would be back before we knew it. Ruby never liked Susan, and I thought she might have contributed to the reason Ruby left, but she still didn't return. None of the girls did. Shaking off the shock of seeing Ruby and ignoring how good she looked, I realize something. Ruby's home, so that must mean that Pru and the other coven members' spell must have worked. I roll my eyes at the thought. They are going to be insufferably smug about it.

I finish throwing all of my things into my truck then pull off my dirty overalls so I'm standing in nothing but my boxer briefs. I wave a hand along my body, and my magic instantly cleans me up. I reach into the back of the truck and pull out a clean shirt and jeans, quickly putting them on before I grab my cell to ring Regan and give him a heads-up on Ruby, but he doesn't answer. I hang up and throw it onto the truck seat. Regan will just have to be surprised.

Climbing into my truck, I pull out of the resort, leaving the gate open, and drive back through town to my workshop. The fall leaves are stunning at this time of year, and tourists usually flock here in droves for the change of season, but this year is different. Everything is different. Everything just feels wrong. You know that lull before a significant storm, the buildup of electricity in the atmosphere, that knowledge that something is about to happen, but you are not sure what? That feeling is what makes me so concerned. Is Ruby's return the catalyst for the coming change? I'm not sure, but I plan to be on guard.

Pulling the truck into the parking space behind my workshop, I turn it off. A distinct odor hangs thick in the air, burning the nostrils with the industrial smell of burning coal and molten iron. The ringing sound of a hammer banging against an anvil can be heard from inside the workshop. Cole must be visiting from the vampire realm. He's the only other person who would be using my workshop. Regan didn't tell me he had come through the portal, but I guess he has a lot of different things on his mind with his staffing struggles.

I leave the vampire to himself. Cole doesn't come through the portal often anymore, and when he does, it's usually to escape a family member or a prospective mate. I'll let him hammer out his frustrations and hopefully convince him to have a pint with me at the pub tonight.

Leaving my truck where it is, I shove my phone into my back pocket and wander over to my mom's ice cream shop. The crackle of fallen leaves under my feet is a loud reminder that winter is coming.

The lack of tourists is evident on Main Street. Usually, it's teeming with families and friends, people eating treats, or carrying bags of items they bought at one of the little stores. Today there are a few people about, but nothing compared to past years.

Arriving at the door of Mom's shop, I push it open and enter. A family stands at the counter—a mom, dad, and their three children who must all be under five. I can see Mom's shop girl, Sheree, waiting while they argue about what flavor of ice cream they are going to pick. She rolls her eyes and sighs out loud with impatience. A frown crosses my face. That's not a great attitude to have when working in the service industry. There is just something about her, something I can't quite work out, a niggle in my chest, but then my brain tells me I'm being ridiculous. She's pretty and fun to be with, so I ignore the feeling in my chest and smooth out my frown as she looks up and notices me waiting.

A big smile crosses her face, and she skips toward me. "Maddock!" she exclaims, planting a kiss on my cheek and throwing her arms around me. "What brings you here today? Did you miss me?"

I extract myself from her hug but smile at her. My body, mind, and heart can't seem to agree on anything, but I shake it off and answer her. "Just here to see Mom, is she around?" She frowns at me in disappointment, but behind her, I can see the family is ready to order, so I turn her around and push her toward them. "Never mind, I'll just go and have a look for myself."

Making my way around the counter, I enter the kitchen area where Mom makes all her ice cream. I see her standing next to one of the big, silver, commercial grade gelato machines. Holding a tub under the nozzle, she coaxes the green ice cream into it, careful not to lose any over the side.

"So is that mint, pistachio, avocado, or some other weird combination? Maybe marijuana?" I ask her, causing her to jump with fright. I dash forward to catch the tub before it drops out of her hands, but she manages to stabilize it herself before looking up at me with a growl.

"Damn it, Maddock, always sneaking up on me. You need a damn bell on your collar! If I didn't know better, I would say you were a vampire or some sort of cat shifter."

I laugh at my mother. "Nope, sorry to disappoint, just a regular witch over here." I look at her sideways. "Unless there is something you are not telling us?"

She finishes up with the ice cream and pulls a lever on the machine to close it before placing the tub on a counter. Wiping her hands on a cloth, she reaches out and pulls me in for a hug. I tower over the woman, have for years, but she still treats me like I'm five.

I love it and return the hug enthusiastically, swinging her around on the spot.

"Put me down, you great oaf," she shouts, swatting me on the shoulder. "Nope, nothing I need to share. You are the spitting image of your father when he was your age." She leans back against the counter.

"Marijuana ice cream? I wonder if we could do it and make it taste good. Maybe Mr. Google can help." She goes over to the whiteboard she uses for her shopping list and adds marijuana to it. "Now, tell me why you are here."

I arch my eyebrow at her. "Can't a son just visit his mom for no reason other than he wants to see her?"

She looks at me shrewdly. "Cut the crap, Maddock. I can see it in your aura, it's practically buzzing. You definitely have a reason to be here, now spill."

"Guess who I just saw driving up to the manor?" She looks at me with exasperation. I'm definitely starting to annoy her. If I'm not careful, cooking implements might start flying at me from all directions like they used to when I was a kid.

She puts her hands on her hips. "I don't know, Maddock, who did you see driving up to the manor?"

I pause for dramatic effect, and a ladle flies toward me from the wall it was hanging on. "Shit!" I exclaim, quickly ducking. "Damn it, Mom, there is no need for that!" She starts growling. "Settle, woman. Are you sure *you're* not a shifter?" This time it's a wooden spoon I have to dodge. I hold my hands out and pause it mid-flight. "Okay, okay, I'll tell you. It was Ruby Miller."

My mom sways on her feet, her normally tan

complexion turning ashen white. A hand comes up to her mouth. "It worked," she whispers, and I nod my head.

"Looks like it," I agree with her, and a huge smile crosses her face.

"Tatiana's coming home?" she asks quietly, but I don't want to get her hopes up too much, so I reply, "Possibly!"

She starts to sob with joy, so I pull her into my arms and let her tears soak into my shirt. *Damn you, Ruby. You better not get her hopes up and then let her down.*

"But you can't tell Pru yet," I tell her hurriedly. "Ruby said they didn't know she was coming, and I don't want you to ruin the surprise. You will just have to hold it in for a couple of hours."

Wiping the tears from her eyes, she nods her head enthusiastically while miming zipping her lips. "I won't say a word until she calls me." I guess that's as good as I will get and quickly agree.

Later, after I've managed to calm Mom down and she gloated for a little while about the spell working, I leave her to google marijuana ice cream recipes and mutter to herself.

I get a hug and another kiss on the cheek from Sheree, even though she has customers waiting, and find myself back on Main Street. I look back toward the workshop, wondering if Cole has finished bashing away his frustrations. I'll give him another half hour.

Wandering in the opposite direction, I go in search of lunch.

Sometime later, with a full belly, I meander back up the street to the workshop, entering through the side doors. I timed it well, because Cole is throwing the molten metal sword, which is glowing bright orange, into the oil trough to quench it. Steam billows and hisses from the trough as oil bubbles up, and a flame flickers across the top as the air takes on a humid feel.

Cole swipes a hand across his sweaty brow as I lean against the doorframe.

"Feel better?" I ask him cautiously.

He grimaces. "Yeah. Sorry, man. My family is driving me batty. It was either come here and bang out a sword or take one and drive it through my brother's chest."

I laugh and walk over to peer at the sword, which is now sitting at the bottom of the trough, cooling. It's a large, double-edged, double-handed broadsword. It has a cross hilt with a decorative flair at the end of the grip. All it needs now is for the handle to be wrapped in leather and polished to a beautiful sheen.

"Nice work! Are you going to finish it today, or are you in a hurry to get home?" I ask him.

He shakes his head. "I'll finish it before I leave, and you can put it in the shop for a tourist to buy." He picks up the tools he left lying around and puts them away.

"Yes, if only we had a few more," I say to him before grabbing a broom and sweeping up the hammer scale left behind. "Feel like grabbing a pint at the Hamster tonight before you head home? You can catch up with some of the guys before you go."

He finishes putting everything away and turns. "Not tonight," he answers with a sigh. "Now that I'm calmer I need to get back and deal with the mess I didn't deal with before. I couldn't be seen ripping heads off, shame really. I'll come back through tomorrow. I'll probably need to drink Joshua's total supply by then." He wipes his hand off on a cloth and throws it on the bench. "See you tomorrow." With a wave of his hand and a burst of wind, he's gone. Damn vampire speed.

CHAPTER
Four

Ruby

Sometime later—a lot longer than ten minutes—I find myself sitting on the outdoor patio overlooking the grounds of the estate. We both have drinks in front of us, and a long overdue conversation is needed. From where we sit, we can see Kady and Kadir chasing Sugar through the orchard that borders the grounds. We have many varieties of trees in the orchard, and due to the coven, they all produce fruit even if they are tropical fruits like mangoes and bananas. Witchy magic can make anything grow.

I see the children trying to reach an apple hanging on a low branch.

Laughing, I gesture to them, watching Kadir lift Kady so she can get the apple. "I think that's the most exercise Sugar's done in years. They are so much like us."

Regan smiles at them then turns back to me, putting his serious face on. "Have you been to see Mom and Dad yet?" he asks.

I shake my head. "No. I came here first. I didn't want Sugar sitting in the carrier, and to be honest, I wasn't sure if I would be welcome."

"Not welcome?" he repeats incredulously. "Why would you think that?"

I take a moment before I answer. "Look, Regan, I know it's been a long time since I've been home. I feel like I've been living life in a fog, and the sun has finally come out and cleared it. I know I've had conversations with Mom and Dad and even you, but I can't actually remember what we talked about. I think I'll make a doctor's appointment and check it out." Taking a sip of my drink, I look at him with tears in my eyes. "I'm so sorry. Can you ever forgive me? I've neglected everyone."

He pulls his chair closer and wraps his arms around me. "Oh, sis, I think you need a long conversation with Mom. She will explain everything. As soon as you finish your drink, jump in the car and go see her. You will feel so much better when you do."

I wipe the tears from my eyes again. I'm sure it

won't be the last time today. "Speaking of cars, when did we get a valet service?"

He gets a sheepish expression and takes a big breath. "Ruby, the manor hasn't been doing so well. In fact, the whole town has been suffering. Julie came up with some new ideas, and we implemented them. That was one."

"And Julie? Where did she come from, and why was a human working at the portal?"

"We have had to look outside town for people to work some of the jobs. The minute someone turns eighteen, they leave. I'm not the only one, most businesses have strangers working for them. The majority are from Kingston and the surrounding areas."

"Okay, okay, I get it. We are desperate. I need to go see Mom and Dad. It doesn't sound like everything that's been happening is natural." I drain the rest of my drink, put the glass onto the table, and stand up. "Wish me luck." I place a kiss on his head and walk out to find where the damn valet put my car.

Less than half an hour later, I pull my Mustang into the driveway of my parents' estate.

The founding members of the Arbor Vitae Coven all have estates on the same street, so all the children of the coven grew up together. I have nine very close girlfriends. The Tempting Ten, they used to call us in high school. I can't, for the life of me, remember when I last spoke to any of them. I really need to do something about that. But parents first.

I stare up at the place I grew up in. Nothing's changed on the outside except Mom has added a few new rose bushes.

The door to my parents' home flies open, crashing against the wall. Standing there with her mouth open and tears building in her eyes is my mother. I study her. The woman is gorgeous. She has thick, flowing auburn hair, striking jade green eyes, and a smattering of freckles across her nose. She is dressed in a fifties style dress, which accentuates her bust and flares out at the waist. My mother is the very image of Suzy Homemaker, and you wouldn't guess the woman is a powerful witch just by looking at her.

She opens her arms wide. "Ruby, my baby, you're back." She rushes toward me, enveloping me in a hug that is bordering on abusive, and the smell of violets hits me as she encloses her arms around me. The comfort of being back in my mom's arms and the smell of my childhood relaxes me instantly. Everything's going to be all right now. We are both sobbing loudly when I hear a voice from inside the house.

"Who is it, Pru? What is that god-awful wailing?"

Alastair Miller asks, wandering out the door holding his newspaper in one hand. His mouth drops open in shock, and he drops the paper when he catches sight of me.

I untangle myself from Mom's embrace, and with her arm around my waist, I wave. "Hi, Dad."

"Pumpkin, you better get yourself in this house and give me a squeeze. I have missed you so much!" he shouts at me as I run up the driveway and throw my arms around him as hard as I can. Mom follows, pulling the door closed behind us. Dad drags me into the living area, and we take a seat on the super comfy couches they have in here. I find myself squished between the two of them, neither letting go of the hands they grabbed hold of. Dad lifts one hand and snaps his fingers, and I can hear the kettle switch on in the kitchen.

As I look at them, all I can do is burst into tears. Sobbing, I throw myself into Mom's lap. "I'm sorry! I don't know why I haven't been here. I don't remember having had a conversation with you or the girls or Regan for a long time. Every time I thought about coming home, something came up. Then Mr. Whitmore just passed away, we just had his funeral. Then Junior demoted me to sales, and he took away my kitchen," I ramble. "Suddenly it was like lightning struck, then instant clarity. I told him to shove it, packed my bags, and here I am. Can you ever forgive me for being such a bad daughter?" Mom coos and strokes my hair as I blurt all this out.

"My sweet girl, hush now, none of this is your fault."

Dad gets up and goes to the kitchen while Mom continues.

"Honestly, nothing is your fault. We need to talk about some things. Let's have a nice cup of tea. I have so much to tell you."

Dad comes out carrying a tray with a teapot and some cups on it. He places it on the coffee table in front of us and pours us all a cup. I take a sip of my tea, the soothing warmth sliding through my body. Feeling calmer, I take a deep breath. "Okay, Mom, tell me what's going on."

"Where to start?" she muses.

"Just tell her everything," Dad says as he munches on a cookie, crumbs falling onto his shirt and then to the couch. Mom frowns at him, and he just smiles sheepishly.

"Did you know that all the oldest girls from the coven left town at the same time? None of them have returned permanently. Their mothers have had to hire people to come in and help run their businesses."

"Yeah. What is that?" I question. "Regan had a stranger working at the manor."

"It seems that all the young people in town are leaving. The minute they hit eighteen, everyone finds something better far away. We have had to advertise in other towns. They are not living here, they boat in every morning, but they have been pushing to move here. You know we don't let outsiders live in town, so we've been putting them off."

"All of the businesses?" I ask her quietly.

"Yes, baby. When Susan ran off, I needed to be there to help Regan with the twins. I couldn't put myself in both places."

I stand up and start pacing. "There's a stranger in my candy shop, making my candy?" I growl.

"Yes, Ruby. I tried to tell you, but it was like you wouldn't hear me. This is what led me to my investigation. That's how I found out you were under a spell."

I collapse back onto the couch, the air whooshing out of me. "A spell?"

"Yes." Mom nods. "All the girls were under a repelling spell. Now that I think about it more, I believe it may be aimed at all the young folk from the town, but we did a counter spell for the coven girls, and I'm guessing it worked now that you are here. We may have to do a whole island spell and lift the contamination."

"Why are you here?" Dad asks. "Not that I'm complaining," he reassures me, "but it is out of the blue."

"When Mr. Whitmore died, I had a sudden urge to come home," I tell him, and Mom gasps before muttering, "Serious consequences," under her breath. She grabs hold of my hand.

"Oh, honey, the counter spell we did said it may have some serious consequences. I'm so sorry."

I just look at her and shake my head. "Mom, Mr. Whitmore had a bad heart, it could have happened at any time." She looks skeptical but doesn't say anything else. Sitting up, I take a deep breath. "Well, I'm here now, and I want my store back. I have so many new ideas, and I have some preexisting orders from the last shop that I need to make. When can we get rid of the new girl?"

"Ruby, don't be like that," Mom scolds. "She has been a great help to your father and me. Now that you are back, Al can finish at the shop too, and she can be your assistant."

Wrinkling up my nose, I take a moment to think about that. "I guess it could work. Is she a supe? Now that I'm back, I want to combine some spells with candy to give the supes a new product range, something they can't get anywhere else. Hopefully that will drum up some new business. Maybe some special ones for humans, too, that could give them things like wings for half an hour or something… I need to think on it. It may be more than they can handle."

Mom claps her hands together with a thrilled look on her face. "I knew this would be the right thing to do. I knew that having the girls back would breathe new life into this old town." She grins at my dad, and he smiles indulgently at her. "I'm not sure if she is a supe, but I guess we could ask the sheriff to have a sniff. His shifter nose is very rarely wrong. Though all supes are supposed to identify themselves when arriving on the island, even if they don't come through the portal."

I shake my head at her. "No, don't worry about it right now, it really doesn't matter. I'll just give her strict instructions to follow for the special candy. Maybe you will need to be eighteen to access it or sign a waiver or something. I'll think about it."

The grin that spreads across my mom's face is positively giddy. "That will be fun, what a great idea." She throws her arms around me. "I'm so glad you are home, Ruby."

I hug her back and then stand up, giving my dad a hug. "I'm off. I need to get myself settled and look for somewhere to live. I can't be a burden on Regan. How about I meet you both at the store at six o'clock tomorrow morning? I need to do an inventory of what we've got and what we need. I have so many ideas. I also brought home samples to show you and add to the menu."

"Ruby, the guest house at the manor is still empty. Why don't you move in there?" my dad suggests. "It needs some work, but it shouldn't take too much."

"What a great idea, I forgot all about the guest cottage. Regan and I used to pretend it was our secret hideout. That's one less thing I have to worry about, thank you." I kiss them both on the cheek and run out of the door of my parents' house. Life is looking up.

That afternoon I find myself standing in front of the manor guest house a little shell-shocked. Turning to look at my brother, I gesture to the building in front of us. "Dad said it needed a little work. That... That is a mess."

It's a replica cottage of the main manor building. The front porch was converted to an enclosed sunroom at some stage in its life, but now all the windows have holes in them. I guess kids have thrown rocks through them over the years. Some are missing whole panes of glass. The front wooden steps are all rotten and falling down, there are shingles missing on the roof, and the ivy doesn't look elegant and refined like the main house, instead appearing wild and unruly.

"Yeah, I don't think he's been out here for a while," he replies sheepishly as he steps up to the front door, slipping a key into the lock. "You can stay at the manor while we get some contractors in to fix it up." We both step inside to the sound of a million mice scattering. I let out a screech as a raccoon scuttles out from under an old couch and races out the front door.

We walk through the sunroom before he unlocks the old front door, and then we step into the great room. I look around the dust-covered surfaces, the smell of mold and mildew causing me to wrinkle my nose. The metal steps spiraling up to the loft have rusted out and look as though they need replacing, and the metal beams need to be looked at by someone who knows what they are doing. All the furniture needs to be tossed, and as I look down at the floor covered in rodent droppings, I decide that will be redone too.

The sagging kitchen cabinets and the crooked, rusted door on the refrigerator tell me so much. I don't even want to look at the bathroom, but I'm a glutton for punishment so I wander in. The bathroom tiles are cracked and covered in mold. There are rust-colored stains on the clawfoot bathtub, which has about two inches of debris strewn brown water in the bottom. I just shake my head, turn around, and walk right out.

"It needs to be gutted," I announce to Regan in disappointment. Looking up at the hole that allows the afternoon light to filter through, I sigh. "This place is not livable."

He just shakes his head at me and raises an eyebrow. "Ruby, Ruby, Ruby," he says in disappointment. "Did you forget you have magic?" With a snap of his fingers, the hole in the roof is fixed. He waves his hand in the direction of the kitchen, and with a flash of light, the kitchen is sparkling and shiny again. The appliances gleam, and I can see my reflection in the metal. He stomps his foot, and the flooring is instantly clean, the wooden floorboards polished to a gleam. He turns and smirks at me.

I slap my hand to my head. "I don't remember the last time I used real magic. I tried to brew a few spells, but they always went wrong."

"Yeah, Mom thinks that might have to do with the spell that was on you. Go on, give it a go."

I turn to the living area. There is a big, open stone fireplace with a huge slab of maple for the mantel, but it's hanging crookedly. The surrounding wall is empty and looks to be stained with something. What do I want it to look like? I think about some things I've pinned on Pinterest and then snap my fingers. With another flash of light, rows of bookshelves appear, surrounding the fireplace, the mantel straight and gleaming. I turn to Regan in excitement. "It worked. Thank God! What a relief."

Suddenly, my head feels a bit light and black spots appear before my eyes. Putting my hands up, I grab hold of Regan.

"Whoa, Ruby! Are you okay?" he asks as he guides me to the front door. "Let's get you some fresh air." We walk out to the car.

"I think not having done any magic for a while is taking its toll on me."

Regan helps me get into the car. "Leave it to me, Ruby. You worry about the store for Mom and Dad, and I'll get the house organized for you. I'll get Maddock to look at the wrought iron steps and the balustrade on the loft as well. We will get that bathroom done, get new furniture, and fix all the windows in the sunroom. Just write me a list of what you want us to do."

With that, I lean over and place a kiss on his cheek. "Thanks, bro." Leaning my head back against the car seat, I close my eyes. It is so great to be home with family and have someone to lean on.

CHAPTER
Five

Ruby

The next morning, I find myself driving down the cobbled main street of town. The trees lining the road are lush with multiple shades of green, red, and brown. The streetlights are starting to switch off in the early morning, the pale yellow light of sunrise breaking the horizon. The smell of exhaust from the Mustang lingers in the air as I park in front of the candy store and hop out of the car. I look up at the building.

The whole street is lined with similar storefronts. They all have stone facades with big display windows in the front, and traditional awnings hang above the doorways of most of the buildings. The one over Candy Connection is striped red and white like a peppermint candy. There is a huge sign above the awning with the words *Candy Connection* written in old-fashioned writing. A faint light can be seen shining in the back of the shop.

I take a deep breath of fresh air, and the distinctive smell of the river prickles in my nose, causing a smile to appear on my face. It's so, so good to be home. I watch as Mom and Dad drive up, park their car next to mine, and jump out. After I give them both a big hug, we walk toward the store. Dad pushes open the front door, and I wait in anticipation for the tinkle of a bell, frowning in disappointment when it doesn't happen. Looking up, I notice the bell above the door is missing. That is the first item on my list, I think as I pull out my iPad, open the notes, and start typing.

Looking around the store, I make more notes. It's rather dark and cluttered, so a few changes are definitely required. More lighting is needed, and maybe the shelves can be painted white with a splash of color for accent. The candy kitchen is in the back, but I want to change that. Perhaps we can put it in front of one of the display windows so people can see when they are walking past.

"Mom, how do you feel about me making some changes? Where I used to work, the kitchen was in the store for everyone to see. People enjoy watching the candy being made, and I found that fresh samples encouraged people to purchase more than they originally wanted."

I'm telling them about the different things I want to do, and they are smiling and nodding, when someone clears a throat behind me. Turning around, I find a woman standing there. She is the woman I fired from the manor. Her blonde hair is up in a bun with a hairnet over it, and she's wearing an apron tied around her waist. There is a look of annoyance on her face, which snaps into a smile as soon as my mom and dad turn around.

"Didn't I fire you from the manor yesterday? What are you doing here?" I ask her.

Mom and Dad both look at me in shock. "What? You fired her?" Mom shrieks.

I hush her with my hand and whisper, "I'll explain later."

"No, she fired my sister," the blonde woman snaps.

"Ruby, this is Jenna Hart. She has been helping us out in the shop for a while. Jenna, this is our daughter Ruby. She is going to take Al's candy making position so he can retire. She's got some big plans. Why don't we all head down the street to Buttered Biscuit and get a coffee and breakfast and talk over the changes?"

Jenna frowns and says, "Sorry, but I've got a batch of turtles that I'm wrapping. I need to get them ready for when the store opens."

"Oh, what a shame," Mom replies. "Next time, okay? We will let you know the plans later. We'll be back in a while." She waves and pops out of the store.

Dad stops and says, "Are we good for stock today, Jenna? I'm going to take the day with Ruby if you're okay with that." He puts his arm around me and hugs me hard. "We've missed her so much, and we have so much to plan. We are going to revitalize this store and get a few more tourists in."

A panicked gleam appears in her eye before it clears, and she smiles blandly at my dad. "That's fine, Mr. Miller. I think we are okay for most things. Enjoy your day with your daughter."

Dad waves goodbye and drags me out of the shop.

"I don't like her, Dad," I say the minute the door closes and we are away from the store. Mom is waiting for us, and she threads her arm through mine.

"Tell us what happened with her sister," Mom demands.

"I found her with her hands on Kady and Kadir. They were noisy, and she was not happy. She left bruises on Kady. She was also very rude to me when I went to check in. Didn't even look at me. We do not want someone like her working for us. The kids were so happy when she left. Apparently she was mean to them all the time," I tell them fiercely, defending my actions.

They just look at each other and laugh. "She was a bit of a sourpuss," Mom remarks.

Dad laughs. "A bit? She kept coming to Regan with all these ideas for the manor. The valet service was one we actually decided to try. No children allowed was one that got shot down instantly. I don't know what she thought, considering the twins live there," he says, shaking his head.

We walk into Buttered Biscuit. I can smell the coffee brewing and the fresh, flaky baked goods sitting in the display cabinet. My stomach rumbles. The bakery/coffee shop is a fantastic place to have breakfast, lunch, or morning tea.

I wave to Beatrix Shadowsoul behind the counter, and she waves back with a huge grin. "Grab a seat, and I'll be with you shortly." We take a seat and have a look at the menu. Beatrix comes bustling over to us with her arms wide open, and I stand up and return her hug.

"Well, thank the goddess. Seeing you is a balm to my soul and gives me hope that Paige will return from Paris soon," she gushes. "Breakfast is on the house today. What can I get you?"

We place our orders, and she returns to the kitchen. As we chat quietly about everything that is going on in town, some of my ideas for the store, and how we can revitalize the town, a steady stream of older locals come in for their morning coffees or pastries.

I wave hello to Taylor Crimson, the town sheriff and an old high school friend.

"Ruby Miller!" he says as he comes over to the table. "You are a sight for sore eyes. I take it this means the spell worked?" he asks, turning to my mom.

She nods. "Yes, have you learned anything from our discussion the other day?"

"Not yet, Pru, but I have a few feelers out. We will get to the bottom of this," he vows, shaking his head.

"Taylor, have you met the woman who is working in the shop with Dad?" I inquire.

"Jenna Hart? Yeah, she and her sister are regulars over at the Hamster." The Laughing Hamster is the local tavern and quite a popular place for young people, or it used to be.

"I thought all the young people in town were leaving." I turn to Mom.

"Yes, but it's all the out-of-towners who are here working that hang out there," she tells me.

I turn back to Taylor. "Don't you think it's weird that all the young people are leaving? Can you tell if Jenna and her sister are supes?"

He frowns at me, shrugging his shoulders. "They don't smell like a vamp, fae, or shifter, but witches don't have a smell either, so they may be human or they may be witches. Who knows?" He turns to

Mom, looking unconcerned. "Will you keep working on the spell for the whole town?"

"Like I explained, the spell we did for the girls had some possible consequences. With so many young people leaving, we can't use that same spell. I'm hoping once a few more of the girls return, we can do a different spell requiring the whole coven, including the husbands and other children. That should be strong enough to break the blanket spell over the town," she explains.

"Great, then I will concentrate on the who, not the what. I hope to see you around, Ruby." He winks at me, grabs his coffee from the counter, and walks out of the bakery. I watch him walk away, the tight fit of his uniform providing a delicious sight. I look up as the door closes. Mom and Dad are watching me— Mom with a sly smile on her face.

"Have you seen Maddock since you've been back? Maybe he can help with updating the shop," she suggests, taking a sip of her coffee, hiding her smile behind the cup.

"Mom, just no. I am not a starry-eyed, sixteen-year-old. And yes, I saw him on the way to the manor yesterday. He did not look happy to see me."

"Yeah, he was disappointed when you didn't come back into town to help Regan when Susan left. He is such a loyal friend. He moved into the manor to help with the twins for a few weeks until Regan came to his senses and realized he was better off without the bitch," Dad tells me.

"I went around one day and found them both passed out on the couch, each with a twin in their arms. They were terrors at three, and the only time we found peace was when they were asleep." Mom chuckles. "He had food and drool smeared all over his shirt, and he was so tired he was drooling in his sleep. He is such a good man. He's going to make someone a great husband one day." She pats my hand, and I panic, waving Beatrix over to change the subject.

"Is Gerald still doing all the cabinet making in town?" I ask her.

She shakes her head. "No, he has slowed down now and is only doing the paperwork. Bram has taken over," she replies. Bram and Paige are her children and friends of mine. Paige is in Paris, attending a pâtissier college, and Bram was apprenticing with his dad when I left.

I pull a pen out of my handbag and write my number on a napkin. "Can you ask him to give me a call? I'm going to need some work done at the shop, and possibly out at the cottage too."

She pats my hand, smiles, and says, "Will do, love. So glad you are home, Ruby."

Sometime later, we walk up the street toward the candy store. As I look around the main strip, a feeling of sadness descends. The sun is shining high in the sky and the temperature is pleasant. Usually the sidewalk would be teeming with visitors and locals, but today there aren't many people around at all. I wave to Jandar, who's riding one of his horses down Main Street, and I can see a few non-locals browsing the storefronts.

The lights in the jewelry store are off, so I turn to Dad. "Why is the light off in Pretty Pieces? There isn't any jewelry in the window either! Is Marie okay?"

A look of sadness crosses his face. "She isn't sick, but she has no inspiration or motivation. She has had depression for the last few months. We are hoping that if and when Temperance comes home, she might snap out of it."

I stop suddenly, anger running through my body. "You know what?" I exclaim. "Enough is enough! I am going to organize the store and the cottage, and if they haven't started to show their faces in town by then, I will start making phone calls. I'm sure none of them realize how bad it's become. Temperance adores her mother. There is no way she wouldn't return if she knew Marie was like that. Someone has a lot to answer for with that spell, and I know ten women who will happily dole out justice."

We walk up to our cars parked in front of Candy Connection. Next door to the candy store is the ice cream shop. Through the window, I see Lucille Crane arguing with a young woman inside. Their voices escalate in volume, and just as we all step toward the entrance, the door flies open and the woman comes stomping out, flipping Lucille the bird. We rush inside. Lucille is slumped in one of the booths with tears flowing down her face. Mom runs up to her and throws her arms around her.

"What was that about, Lucille?" Dad demands. "What did she do? Shall I call the sheriff?"

The sobs lessen, and Lucille blows her nose on a napkin from the table. "That was Sheree. She's been working for me for a couple of weeks, but there is something about her… She's not polite to the customers, she's constantly late, she isn't interested in learning to make the recipes, and every time Maddock comes in, she bats her eyelashes and pushes out her chest. I was telling her she needed to be nicer to the customers and leave Maddock alone because he was spoken for, and she started yelling at me."

My heart drops at the news that Maddock has a

girlfriend, but I ignore it and watch Mom and Dad console Lucille.

"I'm so tired. I don't want to do this on my own anymore," she tells Mom.

"What about Melody Shelly?" I suggest. "She must be about sixteen, so she should still be in town. Maybe she needs a job to earn some extra cash. I know she's not helping Denise because she gets allergies from the fragrances at the chandlery, much to her disappointment."

Lucille's face brightens instantly. "What a great idea, Ruby! I never even thought of Melly. I'll ring Denise and ask now." She bustles out the back, leaving us in her haste to sort out her problems.

I turn to Mom and Dad. "Tatiana will be the first person I call. Her mother needs her." After a brief moment, I add, "And so does her best friend."

CHAPTER
Six

Ruby

L ater that night, I sit in the bar at the manor, enjoying a cocktail made by the bartender. Well, I should be enjoying it, but it tastes a little funny. I eye the bartender sideways, but again, they are not someone I know. The bar is quiet this evening, and it's no wonder if the drinks all taste like mine. Pushing it to the side, I open the notebook I was jotting down ideas in. I have all sorts of ideas for the spell candy, and I want to make sure I get the spells right. Lost in thought, I jolt in surprise when a tiny little body launches itself into my lap.

"Aunt Ruby, it's bedtime, and I need you to read me a story," Kady says, wrapping her little arms around my neck. I close my notebook and put the pen down on top.

"Well, of course you can have a story, Princess Kady." I pick her up and carry her up to her room. I find her brother in bed already, and Sugar is well and truly comfortable at the foot of it.

"Mm-hmm," I mutter. "I see how it is, traitor." She blinks at me and then continues washing her fur.

"Aunt Wuby! I knew you would come. Can you read the story about Sean the seal?" He hands me a book and pats the bed next to him. Sitting, I pull Kady down next to me. It's tight in the bed with the three of us, but they are freshly out of the bath, and they have that fantastic fresh child smell.

I take a deep breath of Kadir's hair, and he looks at me strangely. "Did you sniff me, Aunt Wuby?"

I chuckle sheepishly, nodding my head. "Hush now," I tell him and start the story. By the time I'm finished, they are both out like lights, and Kadir is snoring lightly. I pick Kady up and tuck her into her bed, and as I leave, I switch on the lamp between their beds before turning off the overhead light, then I close the door slightly.

Their living area is separate from the rest of the manor, and Regan is still dealing with manor business. The kids have an intercom in case they wake and need him, but I decide to wait until he returns. I go to take out my notebook and realize I left it down in the bar. Running downstairs quickly, I find it's still there but it's open, and the pen is sitting on the side. I'm sure I closed it and left the pen on top. Looking around, I see no one but the bartender. He is polishing glasses behind the bar. Picking up my stuff, I head back up to Regan's place. Maybe the wind blew it open, but as I turn around to check, I see none of the windows are ajar.

I head back upstairs to wait for Regan.

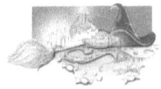

A gentle shaking wakes me from my slumber. I fell asleep on the couch, and the drool sliding down my cheek is cold and wet. Reaching up, I wipe it away with the back of my hand, slurping a little as I sit up.

"Real classy, sis." Regan watches me with laughter in his eyes from his seat on the other couch. He has dark shadows under his eyes and a look of exhaustion on his face.

"What's wrong, Regan? You look like shit."

He blows out a deep breath, his head falling back onto the couch. "Don't sugarcoat it or anything," he says sarcastically. "Even with the lack of visitors, I'm still short-staffed. Julie upset a lot of my staff members, and they quit and left town before I realized what was happening. The valet is Julie's brother, and the bartender, Zach, is a friend of hers. I have one housekeeper and one receptionist left, and they are also friends of Julie's and live off the island. I have no night staff, and because of this, no room service to offer. Mom has been running the kitchen while trying to wrangle the twins. It's not an easy job. And the icing on the cake? I just got a call from the mayor. Lucas says the council has received an application from a company wanting to build a new hotel here in Morbank. I just feel like everything has been so hard since Susan left. I could do with a break." The look of defeat on his face is heartbreaking.

"Well, Dad's retiring now, so I'm sure he will help out here for a while. Also, it's summer, so what about putting up a notice at Buttered Biscuit and on the town Facebook page? I'm sure there are a whole heap of teenagers needing summer jobs. That gives us a couple of months to get the young adults to return to town. Also, maybe you can advertise in some of the realms. There may be some supes who want a change of pace. They can come in and out of the portal if they don't want to move into town."

The look of hope on his face is priceless. "Why didn't I think of those things?"

"Sometimes, when you get bogged down by your problems, a fresh perspective helps." I smile at him and stand up. "Alright, I need to go to bed. I'm meeting Bram at the store in the morning to go over the changes I want."

Regan stands up with me. "Great, he's coming out to the cottage in the afternoon to do some work out here too. I've got the glazier coming to do some magic on the windows in the sunroom, and I saw the Pinterest pics you sent me for the bathroom, so I'll get that done as well. It will be finished before you know it."

"Awesome," I reply. "Is there any way we can add a spare bedroom to the back? I want somewhere for the twins to be able to sleep when they come visit me."

The smile he gives me lights up his face. "They will be thrilled. We will work it out somehow."

I give him a kiss on the cheek and head to my bedroom. I do my pre-bed routine and then climb into the soft sheets of my bed. There is so much to do tomorrow, but today has been exhausting, and before I know it, I'm out like a light.

The next day I meet Bram at the store. After a hug and a quick catch up on our lives, I explain what I want done. We discuss walls being torn down, new fixtures, and shelving. I show him where I want the candy kitchen to be located. All the while, Jenna alternates between throwing dirty looks at me and fluttering her eyelashes and flirting with Bram. It's weird. I want to know what her problem is. As soon as I can find a reason to get rid of her, she will be gone too.

"Jenna, why don't you take a couple of days off?" I suggest to her, and the scowl on her face increases. "The shop is going to be closed for a week while we get all these changes made, so you may as well take the time too." Then I have an idea. "Unless you want to keep working? Regan is a little short-staffed out at the manor. I can make a call and see if he can use you."

Her eyes light up, and a devious look crosses her face. I need to watch this girl closely. "That would be great, Ruby. We really need the money now that Julie's not working," she says, and a stab of guilt hits me, but then I remember the marks on Kady and I get over it.

"Great, why don't you take the rest of the day off? I'll get Regan to call you with your times."

She grabs her purse, and with a wave and a wink to Bram, she saunters out the door. I look up at the space where the doorbell used to hang, missing the sound. Bram notices my look.

"She got rid of it! Claimed the ringing gave her a headache. Your dad felt sorry for her, so he never said anything."

I purse my lips in annoyance. "Well, that's one of the first things to go back," I reply with a wink. "It may encourage her to quit, and I won't have to figure out a way to get her to leave."

He laughs. "Well, good luck to you. I'm heading out to the manor now to see Regan and what work needs to be done with the cottage. I'll pull in Dad and his magic to help us so we can get these jobs done as soon as possible. You may want to talk to Joshua about getting some beer barrels to use for displays. Probably new ones, though, as used ones will smell like beer, and that won't go well with the scents in here," he comments, wrinkling his nose.

I laugh and nod. "I thought I might go to the Hamster tonight for a drink. Is he there most nights?"

Bram nods. "Yes, either he or his partner will be there."

I raise my eyebrows in question. "Partner? He's in a relationship?" Joshua was a real player in high school. He had many boyfriends and girlfriends, but no one he was serious about.

"Yeah, Galan is fae. Joshua met him when he went to the fae realm to inquire about importing fairy wine to sell through the pub. He and Joshua have been together ever since. Josh is smitten."

"Wow! I can't wait to meet the man Josh is into. He must be something special to get him to settle down. Is he right for him?"

"Just you wait," he says. "I'm completely hetero, but even I think the man is pretty. It must be a fae thing. They have all got that ethereal quality, and yes, he seems equally as smitten." He goes to leave, but I remember something else.

"Oh hey, listen. The other thing I want is a wrought iron tree in the corner over there." I point to where I want it. "Sort of a nod to the coven. I want holes drilled into it, and I'll use it to display lollipops. I think the kids will get a kick out of it."

He looks a little uncomfortable and fidgets a bit.

"What, Bram? Just spit it out," I demand.

"Well, you'll have to see the blacksmith for that," he says quietly, and my heart drops.

"Fuck. But can you maybe—"

"Good luck with that," he says, cutting me off. Picking up his tape measure, pen, and paper, he races to the door and disappears.

"Damn it!" I yell as I watch him get into his truck and drive away.

Walking to the door, I look up. With a snap of my fingers, a little bell appears above the door. I grab the handle and pull it open. A bright little tinkle sounds throughout the shop and I smile. At least something has been set right. Now to go and speak to the black-smith. The bottom drops out of my stomach, and nerves cause my heart to race. Well, I'm going to blame the nerves.

Closing and locking the door behind me, I pull my phone out of my pocket and dial Regan as I walk down Main Street toward the blacksmith.

"Ruby! You've got some explaining to do!" Regan growls at me.

"Crap, is she there already? I told her to take the rest of the day off and I would give you a call."

"Not what happened," he growls again. *Well shit!* He's really annoyed.

"Look, I don't need her this week, and you do. I don't know, put her in housekeeping or something. Then you won't have to deal with her. Or… I know… get her to mow the grounds. That will keep her busy for ages." I giggle at my suggestion.

He laughs. "That's actually not a bad idea. Alright, thanks, I'll find a use for her."

"Actually, that's not the only' reason I called," I say quickly before he can hang up.

"What do you want?" he asks suspiciously.

"Well, I need a wrought iron tree made, and I was hoping—"

"No, no, no," he interrupts. "You can deal with that yourself."

"But Regan," I whine, "he's your best friend, and maybe you could explain about the spell and everything."

"No! I'm not getting involved, and he knows about the spell anyway." He hangs up without saying goodbye.

I look at the phone in shock. *Asshole!* And after I just helped him. I shove my phone back into my pocket and look up. The noise registers in my ears, and I realize I'm standing in front of the blacksmith.

The continuous sound of a hammer on the anvil rings out, echoing through the air. The forge fan roars as it blasts the heat higher, and sweat starts to pebble across my brow. I watch as the blacksmith walks toward a large black horse tied to the hitching rail, lifts its hoof, and presses the shoe down. The hoof sizzles, and the smell of burnt horse hoof registers in my brain. The scent is pungent and unattractive, unlike the man doing the burning. Maddock stands there, holding up the huge hoof, as smoke wafts up. A drop of sweat rolls down his neck and disappears under the neckline of his shirt. After a minute, he pulls the shoe off the hoof and then throws it into a trough of water next to the hitching post. The water hisses, and steam billows upwards. He stands upright and places his hands on his back, arching and stretching it out, a groan echoing from him.

"Damn it! Why doesn't he have a beer gut?" I whisper to myself, checking to make sure I'm not drooling again.

The man holding the horse looks up and chuckles, and Maddock turns to see what he is laughing at. Damn it again! Elves and their hearing. Walking over to them, I reach out and run my hand over the smooth, shiny muzzle of the beautiful animal in front of me—the horse, not Maddock.

"Hey, guys. Jandar, who is this beauty?" I ask the blond-haired elf.

His aristocratic features stretch wide across his face with a grin, and his crystal blue eyes sparkle with mirth. "Hello, Ruby." He half bows in greeting. "It is lovely to see you again. This is Natasha."

I giggle quietly, and he blushes good-naturedly.

"What are you laughing at?" Maddock growls at me. "There's nothing funny about the name."

I raise my eyebrow at him. "Do you know how he names his horses, Maddock?" I ask him caustically, and he shakes his head. "What are his other horses' names?" I prompt.

"Well, there's Bruce, Tony, Thor, Cap…" He trails off and looks at Jandar. "Really?" he asks.

Jandar has a sheepish look on his face.

"Yes, really. They are all named after comic heroes. He also has a Logan and Storm. This must be Natasha Romanoff, better known as Black Widow. She's lovely, Jandar, great name. One of my favorite characters. You know I'm a huge movie nerd too, so no shaming here." I give the horse a pat and turn to Maddock. "Listen, I need something made for the store, and Bram told me you were the one to speak to about it."

He frowns at me, picks up a hammer and nails, and places a few between his lips. Maddock reaches into the trough and pulls out the shoe. Lifting the horse's hoof, he starts to hammer it on. "I'm busy," he grunts through a mouthful of nails.

I cross my arms and tap my foot. "Well, when then?" I ask him crossly. He puts the hoof down, removes the nails from his mouth, and looks at me.

"Listen, Ruby, if it were up to me? Never!"

His answer stuns me. I glance at Jandar, who appears as amazed as I feel, and then look back at Maddock, tears welling in my eyes.

"But Regan is my best friend, and he asked for my help, so I am going out to the cottage this afternoon to see what he needs. I can listen to you then." He walks back toward the forge and picks up another shoe out of the fire with a pair of tongs and starts banging away.

"Fine." Trying not to let my hurt show, I wave goodbye to Jandar and give Natasha one more pat. "See you later, Jandar. We must catch up soon. I'll make some peppermints for the ponies when I get the store up and running."

He smiles at me sympathetically. "That would be great, Ruby, thanks. They will love it."

Turning, I walk back to the shop with tears streaming down my face. The sadness in my heart is suffocating. He is so mad at something I had no control over, and I have no idea how to fix it.

CHAPTER
Seven

Maddock

I don't watch Ruby walk away. I know I hurt her, but I can't bring myself to give a shit. Looking up from the anvil, I see Jandar frowning at me. "What?" I grunt at him before continuing to hammer the shoe into shape.

"What in the world was that?" he asks incredulously. "You guys used to be such good friends. The four musketeers. We had a pool in high school that you would end up together."

I cringe at the thought. "Everyone grows up, man. She is not the girl I knew. The Ruby I knew wouldn't have left her brother hanging when his wife left him.

She wouldn't have left her parents in the lurch with the shop either. Every one of those girls has become selfish, and I really don't want anything to do with any of them." The words coming out of my mouth feel wrong, and my heart aches at the callousness of them, but I can't seem to stop it.

Jandar shakes his head at me. "I don't know what is wrong with you, man, but I think you're being unreasonable. Think very carefully before you say or do something you can't undo."

The silence that surrounds us as I finish shoeing his horse is uncomfortable. Elves are stoic creatures, and once they have said their piece, they let it go. I can feel his disappointment, it's almost tangible. We've been friends for years, and he always liked Ruby.

Dropping the horse's last hoof, I give her a pat on the rump and put the rasp I was using away. Jandar shakes my hand and politely wishes me a good day before vaulting onto Natasha's back and riding off toward his ranch. Watching him ride away, I feel nothing, no guilt or regret, at what I just said to him or his reaction.

Grabbing a broom, I sweep up the mess and put away the other tools I used before heading inside the workshop.

We are located in one of the original stone buildings on the island. Half is a workshop with two forges, one a traditional wood forge with accompanying bellows to push the heat higher, and the other a more modern gas forge. On one wall are all the tools involved with the various projects we undertake. There are different types of hammers, punches, tongs, files, and much more. Two big anvils sit mounted on stone blocks in the middle of the workshop.

My father taught me everything I know. He's cut back on work hours now but still comes in to play. I think it's because Mom gets sick of him and kicks him out. Though now that Alistair is going to retire, I suppose they will spend as much time golfing and fishing together as they can.

On the other side of the building is the showroom. If the smithy is dusty and dirty, then the showroom is in pristine condition, showcasing various medieval weapons, suits of armor, swords, shields, and daggers. Strategically placed lighting and classy display cases add to the overall aesthetic.

Removing my dirty overalls in the workshop and hanging them on a hook, I make my way through the showroom to the office. The showroom is open to the public, but it's not like we're busy. Without the tourists, business has dropped off.

Sitting down in the office chair, I turn on the computer. I need to do some ordering for a project I have coming up. I've been commissioned to forge *something* for an elven prince who will be crowned sometime next year. It's a gift from the coven to the future king, but I'm not sure what I'm going to craft yet. I pull a couple of books down off the shelf to look through for inspiration. It needs to have meaning and promote good relations between the coven and the fae realm. Just recently, things have become strained between our coven and many of the realm races.

Maybe I can make a suit of armor and weave in some spells. Or an impenetrable shield. Or a bow whose arrows never miss. Shaking my head in frustration, I scrap those ideas. I'm sure elves already have those types of things. Maybe I need to talk to Jandar. He can give me an idea. Or Galan.

A noise in the showroom catches my ear. Did someone knock something over? I listen, but it doesn't happen again. Shrugging, I go back to my book, but a short time later, a sound in the doorway catches my attention. Looking up, I see Sheree draped across the doorframe.

"Hi there, handsome, you look like you could use a break." She's holding out a bag from Buttered Biscuit. "I picked up some lunch for you from that place you like so much," she says, screwing up her nose. Sheree has made it very clear how substandard she feels everything is on this island.

I push my chair back from the desk. "Hey, Sheree. Did Mom give you lunch off?"

Again, she screws up her nose. "No, she fired me yesterday," she spits out.

Surprised doesn't even begin to cover how I feel. "Oh, why? That's not like Mom."

Sauntering over to me, she puts my lunch bag on the desk then comes around to my side. She swivels my chair to face her and straddles my lap. "Let's not talk about that now." Her lips meet mine. She kisses me, and I feel nothing, but I kiss her back anyway. Her bottom wriggles against my lap, but my cock doesn't even twitch in excitement. Her tongue feels like a slobbery wet slug in my mouth. I am going through the motions, but I have no real reason why. It's like someone else is in control of my body. Her hand reaches down, and she starts to unzip my jeans, and I finally get the will to push her away.

"What do you mean Mom fired you?" I ask as she pouts at me. She gets up and paces around the office.

"Your mom is obsessed with customer service. She said I was rude to the customers," she scoffs, gesturing with her hands. "She said that I needed to keep my eyes and hands off of you when you came into the shop. That you were a taken man. I guess we just proved how wrong she is," she says smugly.

A small smile crosses my face as I think about all the times Mom and Pru schemed to put Ruby and me together. I definitely never objected, but it never developed into anything but a good friendship either, much to my disappointment. She left before we could become more.

Sheree's hand brushes against my shoulder, and a cold feeling encompasses my body. My smile drops, and a frown takes its place. "Huh, she was always delusional. Ruby and I never would have worked out. She's just too selfish for me."

I hear myself say the words, but again they feel wrong. Shaking my head, I try to clear it, but Sheree has her hand on my zipper and has it halfway down now. Her mouth is back on mine, and the rasping noise of the zipper opening thunders through the otherwise silent office. She gets it all the way open, and before I know it, her mouth leaves mine and she's on her knees in front of me. She reaches into my boxers, wearing a satisfied smile on her face, before dragging her tongue across her lips in anticipation. Before she can take out my cock, however, and put it in her mouth, the sound of a throat clearing behind me draws my attention. Shaking my head in confusion and embarrassment at almost being caught, I push her away and zip up my jeans. What was I thinking, letting her do that at my place of business?

Turning around, I see Regan in the doorway watching me with confusion and anger in his eyes. "Sorry, I didn't know you had company," he says with derision. "I thought we were heading out to Ruby's this afternoon to fix up her loft so she has somewhere she can sleep."

Sheree's eyes narrow at his comment. She is now on her feet, standing next to me, and she runs her hand over my arm. "But, baby, I brought you lunch, and then we were going to have dessert." She winks suggestively but pouts as I shake my head.

Giving her a kiss on her cheek, I put my hand on her back and walk her out to the showroom. "Sorry, Sheree. I promised Regan I would help him this afternoon, and I forgot all about it. How about we see each other later? We are going to the Hamster for a beer tonight. We can meet there." Her eyes light up, and she nods her head. Waving goodbye, she leaves, and I slump against a display case.

"Well, that looked cozy," Regan comments sarcastically.

Running my hands through my hair, I blow out a big breath. "Leave it, man. I'm a big boy, I can look after myself."

"No, I won't," he snaps. "What is going on with you? Why are you doing this? I thought Ruby was it for you, man. You used to tell me all the time how you were just waiting for her to come home. You were *happily* waiting for her. What the hell happened? She's back, but you don't seem to care one bit. I know you were disappointed that she was away for so long, but it turns out there are reasons."

"Too little too late," I tell him as that cold feeling in my chest takes root. "I'm with Sheree now. Come on, let's get this over with. The less time I spend with your sister, the better."

Regan looks like I punched him in the gut. Grabbing the keys to my truck, I walk out the front door. Regan follows behind, still speechless. In awkward silence, we climb into my truck and head out to the manor guesthouse.

CHAPTER
Eight

Ruby

That afternoon, I find myself standing in the new, shiny sunroom at the cottage. The panes of glass have all been replaced and are sparkling clean and crystal clear. On one side of the door is a sitting area with a couple of comfy chairs, a coffee table, and a lamp. It's a cozy space where I can curl up with a good book during the day. At the other end of the sunroom, I set up an area for selling the spelled candy I am going to make for the supernatural clients.

Because of the strength of the spelled candy, we don't want humans buying it in case they have a terrible reaction, so I will advertise and be open for two hours in the evening from home. Maybe, later on, I can talk to the other businesses and suggest they offer spelled products too.

Apart from a small counter for ringing up transactions, I haven't made any decision on shop furnishings for the other end of the sunroom. I'm not entirely sure of the list of products I'm going to offer yet, since I need to experiment a bit. I asked Regan to make my kitchen counter marble and put a gas stove in for me so I can make little batches of candy at home too. A small warming table on rollers completes the setup. My kitchen rocks. I'm so happy with it.

The rest of my house is also finished apart from the loft. My bathroom is a slice of paradise. The old porcelain claw-foot bath has been replaced by a large grotto-like shower. There are heads hidden in rock walls on three sides, as well as a rainfall head on top. It's programmable, and there's an awesome seat on one end where I can sit to shave my legs. Ferns are planted in ledges and crevices, making it look like a secret oasis. I love it. I also don't need a bathtub anymore, because I now have a spa out on the back deck.

Waiting for Regan and Maddock to come by, I think about the types of spells I can add to candy. They are going to fix the staircase up to the loft, and Maddock will assess the beams for stress fractures or rust or something. I'm not entirely sure what, but Regan insists Maddock needs to do it.

For the special candy for humans, I'm going to create a batch with a spell to give them fairy wings. It will last for an hour, and they won't be able to lift off the ground more than a couple of feet since I don't want anyone suing me for damage.

The next one will be the ability to run super fast. Again, it will only last an hour. The last one I have come up with will give humans the ability to change their hair color continuously for twenty-four hours.

I've also got some adult only ideas that will work for both humans and supes. There is the candy that works like Viagra, creating a two hour hard-on, one that makes sexual fluid taste like your favorite flavor, and an illusion spell for couples. The last one will make your partner look like your celebrity crush, just for fun. Those will do to start, and we will add more if they are popular or we get special requests.

I have a small batch of sugar, glucose, and water on the stove. The spelled candy will be like hard candy, and I'll make them different colors so we'll know the various spells. The thermometer sits in the pan, waiting for it to get to the right temperature, while I decide on the color and flavor I'm going to use. I also have my laptop open, checking my social media and emails. I received a few from previous customers making inquiries. There are also a couple of emails from Junior accusing me of stealing all his customers and destroying his business, threatening to sue me. I delete them and silently wish him luck. He has no leg to stand on.

I reply to a few emails, and I am just about to check the temperature of the boiling sugar when there is a knock on the door. Placing a pause spell on the candy so the sugar doesn't burn, I go to check the door. Just as I get to the sunroom, Regan and Maddock come walking through.

"Hey, sis. What's that smell? Are you cooking something?" he asks, giving me a kiss and walking through to the kitchen. Maddock and I nod awkwardly to each other and follow after him.

"Thanks so much for all your and Bram's work today. The house looks amazing, and once the loft is done, I'll be out of your hair," I tell my brother as he pulls open the fridge and grabs a couple of beers, handing one to Maddock. Huh, Regan must have stocked them earlier.

"You know you are always welcome at the manor. It is half yours, and the kids love having you around."

I smile at him. "The new bedroom out the back is amazing, the kids are going to love it. I can't wait to have them over."

He laughs. "Maybe not when you don't get any sleep because they keep you up all night."

"The added deck was a great surprise, thank you. I won't miss having a bath with the hot tub on the deck. The best part of not living close to the manor and having no neighbors is that I don't even need to use a suit." I wink at him, and both he and Maddock end up spitting out their beer in surprise. I point to the staircase. "When you're done with the loft, Maddock, I've got a drawing of the piece I need made for the shop, if you wouldn't mind having a look," I say to him, knowing he won't want to refuse around Regan.

My hunch about Regan not knowing how pissed he is at me pays off when he scowls at me behind Regan's back. "Why would he mind?" Regan asks, raising his eyebrows and turning to look at Maddock. "Of course he will have a look."

I decide to throw him a bone. I can be petty, but he is Regan's friend. "I just know how busy he is, Regan, and I wasn't sure if he would have the time."

"Nonsense! Let's get this loft done, and then you can show him." He puts his beer down and walks to and up the spiral staircase. Maddock follows him, and I go back to my candy. I can hear them having a low volume conversation. It sounds like they are arguing, but to be able to find out for sure, I would have to walk out into the middle of the living room and look up at the loft. There is no subtle way to do it, so I just leave them be. I could perform a volume spell, but both of them would feel it.

I leave the candy paused. Once it's ready, it needs constant attention until it's finished, and I don't want to be interrupted by the guys. Looking at my empty, sad bookcases, I open a new browser on my laptop and load Amazon. I have a few books in my bag at the manor but not enough to fill it. I spend the next half hour buying more books than I should.

I look up when I feel a wave of magic from the loft. I can tell it's Maddock's from the way it feels. It's strong, hard, and has a cold bite of steel.

Witches and warlocks can perform most magics. Did you ever watch that old seventies television show *Bewitched*, where Samantha could conjure anything with a wiggle of her nose? It's just like that, but most of us don't wiggle our noses. We can also brew potions and chant spells if we need to break a curse or another spell. Some witches also specialize in a branch of magic. The males in Maddock's family have always been good with metal elements, so blacksmithing and weapons have always been a big part of their lives. Maddock's father makes the most elegant but deadly weapons, and before I left, Maddock was heading in the same direction. They sell them to collectors. I have a beautiful dagger he gave me for my eighteenth birthday.

The magic wave continues for about twenty minutes, and Regan's magic eventually joins in. It finally cuts off, and they both come clattering down a fully restored spiral staircase. I walk out and have a look. The stairs and balustrade are shiny and solid black wrought iron again, and the broken rusty sections are gone. I can't see what else they have done, as the rest of the bedroom is set farther back, so I will check it out when they leave.

"All done, Ruby," Regan says. "Maddock does great work."

"Thank you," I tell him gratefully and smile. He just grunts and picks up the beer he left behind. Regan frowns at him and opens his mouth to say something, but his phone rings. He pulls it out of his pocket and swipes his finger across the screen.

"Slow down, Jenna, I can't understand you." He pauses. "They did what?" he shouts, leaping up from the counter where he was sitting. "I'll be right there." He hangs up, shoving his phone in his pocket. "I've got to go. The kids locked Jenna in the attic, and she can't get out. She said it was lucky she had her phone in her pocket. She thinks they thought she was Julie."

I frown at him. "That doesn't sound like them. Sure, they are mischievous, but they are not nasty."

He shrugs his shoulders. "I can ask them later with a truth spell if I need to, but I've got to go sort it out." He slaps Maddock's hand. "I'll see you later, bro." He gives me a kiss on the cheek and off he goes.

We look at each other awkwardly. Maddock takes a deep breath before letting it out slowly. "I'm sorry, Ruby. I've been unfair."

My mouth drops open, and I reach out a hand for a seat before plopping down on one of the stools.

"I was furious when Susan ran out on Regan. He

was heartbroken, but I knew everything would be okay because you would come home and fix everything like you used to when we were younger. You always had a plan. But then you didn't, and things just kept getting worse in town." He runs a hand through his hair in frustration. "Tatiana is also gone, and Mom needs her, and so in my mind, you were both being selfish and neglectful. It was easier to be upset with you than to think that there might actually be a reason you weren't coming home." He looks at me with regret in his eyes. "Regan just told me all about the spell. Mom mentioned something, but no details though. He said that the coven has been trying to keep it quiet so people don't panic. I'm sorry I've mistreated you since you've been home. I took my anger out on you. Can you forgive me?" He has a pleading look in his eyes. "I spoke to Mom, and she told me you temporarily solved her staffing problem for the summer. She spoke to Melody, and she starts tomorrow."

My heart is beating a million miles an hour, and although I felt hurt at the time, there is no way I'm not going to forgive him. Maybe we can hug it out and I can cop a feel, but I'm going to play hard to get. "I was very hurt by your reaction, Maddock. I thought we were friends. We were the four musketeers—you, me, Regan, and Tats," I murmur with real sadness in my voice. "For you to think I would be so deliberately neglectful is devastating."

At this comment, something flashes in my brain, and I start thinking about it some more. Making a guess, I put my hands out and feel his aura for spells. Sure enough, I can feel the malignant, slimy feeling of a negativity spell. The bottom drops out of my stomach.

"Well shit, Maddock! There's actually something here." His eyes widen in panic. "You have a spell on you. What you and Regan just did must have bumped it a bit. It was well hidden."

Going over to the cupboard, I pull out a sage and lavender smudge stick and the lighter I saw earlier when exploring the cabinets. Lighting it, I start waving it around him while chanting a spell breaker. A flash of light and a wave of energy signals the spell breaking. I feel the essence of the witch who cast it, realizing I will recognize the caster if they ever cast around me.

I look at Maddock, and he appears like he has been punched in the gut. A light appears in his eyes, and he takes two steps before wrapping his arms around me and pulling me against his hard chest, holding tight. He nuzzles his face against my hair and breathes deeply. "Ruby, I've missed you so much. Thank God you're home." He rubs his hands up and down my back.

Holy shitake mushrooms. My breasts are smooshed against him, my nipples pebbling at the contact. Slowly wrapping my arms around him, I relish the feeling of being in his arms. I've always dreamed of being held by Maddock like this. Breathing deeply, I smell the smoky, irony smell on his clothes, feeling happier than I have in a long time.

His arms drop and he steps back, rerunning his hand through his hair. I check the front of his shirt to make sure I haven't left any drool on it, and yep, we're good.

"Thanks for that. It's like I had a black cloud surrounding me." With that comment, his eyes wander up and down my body like he is seeing me for the first time. "You are looking really good, Red." He winks at me then walks out the door, whistling. "I'll be seeing you real soon, Ruby," he shouts over his shoulder.

Whoa, that was interesting. I snap my fingers and a fan appears on the counter. Putting my head in front of it, I turn it on and let the breeze cool me down.

I glance between the pot paused on the stove and the spiral staircase. The struggle is real. The desire to see what my bedroom looks like wins, and I run up the stairs to see what the guys have done to my sleeping area.

My mouth drops open in shock. The bedroom is a sensual delight. The sloped walls are paneled pine stained in a vibrant walnut color. There are two large windows built into the walls that run the length of the space, letting in ample light. I can see the green foliage of the trees through them, but it is indistinct due to the textured glass, allowing privacy from the birds.

The triangular wall at the back of the room is also paneled with the same wood, with built-in shelves for books and knickknacks. I can see Regan has put my spell books on there, and there is a plant on each end. Hopefully they are spelled to take care of themselves, because although I'm a wonder with sugar, I have a slightly black thumb.

My eyes are drawn to the luscious bed. The mattress is a large California king and the platform it sits on is lit underneath to make it look like it's floating on air. Plush cushions are stacked up at the head of the bed, and the downy quilt looks like a cloud. Along both walls are low, built-in cupboards for my clothing. Looking up, I notice wrought iron beams running across the roof. They support a chandelier that is a feast of twists and turns, and fake candle globes flicker sensual shadows in the darkened corners.

I nudge my shoes off and throw myself onto the bed, rolling around in joy and delight. What were the guys thinking, creating me such a sexy bedroom? Just as I think this, a piece of paper appears out of thin air above me and flutters down, landing on my chest. I sit up and read what it says.

Ruby,

Hopefully this gets Maddock thinking about you and bed in the same sentence. I nudged him in your direction, but there is also someone else sniffing around. Let's hope he pulls his head out of his ass. I know you have liked him for a long time, and my bet is on you.

Regan

PS. No details please.

PPS. I wouldn't be opposed to a niece or nephew myself.

PPPS. Don't forget to warn him we tend to come in multiples.

My brother, my champion. I guess I never was very subtle about my feelings. Being my twin, Regan sometimes caught those emotions emitting from me if I didn't have them locked down tight. Puberty for the two of us was not always a bundle of laughs. My brother was a horny teenager, and it often carried through the twin link.

Flopping back on my bed, I smile up at the roof. Things are starting to look up.

CHAPTER
Nine

Ruby

After making a few sample batches of spelled sweets, I decide to head to the Hamster. Taking a shower, I wash my hair and shave all my bits, dressing in a pair of skinny jeans that make my bum look amazing and a tight, low-cut top that shows off the girls. Finding my favorite pair of knee-high heeled boots, I pull them on and grab my leather jacket. I walk out the door of the cottage into the sunroom and find Sugar on one of the comfy chairs.

"Hello, traitor. Decided to come home, did you? What's wrong, didn't they feed you?" She just looks at me with derision and goes back to licking her butt.

Hmmm, she does an awful lot of that. Maybe I need to get some worm tablets.

Heading outside, I tug the door shut behind me, jump into the Mustang, and drive over to the Laughing Hamster. As I pull into the spacious parking lot, I notice it's only about a quarter full. The tavern is built from the same stone as the manor, and it has cute little windowpanes with lead lighting in them depicting different scenes. Magic has infused the Hamster over the years. Based on the pub's mood, the views will change to reflect it. I take a good look at what it's showing at the moment—scenes of empty streets, empty stores, and an empty Hamster. Wow, it must be really sad. As I open the big wooden door, I put my hand on the doorframe and send good thoughts and love vibes through to the Hamster. The lights illuminating the inside of the bar are dull and dim, but they brighten minutely with my actions.

Standing just inside the doorway, I take a look around. Running down one long side is a wooden bar that is scratched and scarred with time and use, but it is lovingly polished and wiped to a shine. There are beer taps dotted down its length, a few with recognizable commercial beer signs and some with the Hamster logo. The Laughing Hamster is not only the local watering hole, but it is a microbrewery with an exclusive range of beers. It's ran and managed by the Woods family, also members of the coven.

On the other side of the tavern, tables and booths are scattered around. A third are filled with people chatting and having a good time. Toward the back of the bar, I see the fireplace, which is unlit due to the still mild temperatures of early fall. A new addition I notice on the left side opposite the bar is a wine corner. It's a small, intimate bar set in front of racks of bottled wines, with glasses hanging on rails above head height. Some couches are placed in front of it, giving the area an intimate, cozy feeling.

I wander over and take a seat on one of the stools at the bar and read the colorful cocktail menu, which is on a chalkboard above the bar.

I giggle at the names of the cocktails—Sex on the Hamster, Hamsterpolitan, Hamstini, Mohamster—but there is one of never heard of, the Panty Hamster, with Jägermeister, melon liqueur, raspberry liqueur, and cranberry juice. I wrinkle my nose as a shadow appears next to me and a deep voice says, "Don't knock it until you try it, Ruby."

I look up and smile at Joshua Woods, another good friend of ours growing up.

I lean over the bar, grab him by his shirt, pull him toward me, and smack a massive kiss on his cheek. "I don't know, Joshie, sounds a bit gay." I wink at him as I sit back on my stool.

He throws a smirk my way as he picks up a cocktail shaker and starts to add things to it. "Oh no, Ruby, this drink is for everybody." He pours a dark purple mess into a martini glass, throws a frangipani flower onto it for garnish, and places it in front of me with a flourish. "The Panty Hamster, a cornucopia of alcoholic delight, is guaranteed to not only taste amazing but also guaranteed to drop your panties after a few too." He grins at me. "They are very popular with young males buying for their dates."

I pick up the glass and take a sip, bracing myself for the herby goodness that is Jäger, but instead of the abrasive biting sharpness I expect, it's sweet and smooth, and the icy goodness slides delightfully down my throat.

"Whoa, that is good," I comment as he throws the shaker he used into a sink behind the bar. He comes back to stand in front of one of the taps and pours himself a draft. There is a cute laughing hamster on the tap, and the words *pale ale*.

He places it down next to mine, then he comes around to my side of the bar and pulls me into a big hug. "Missed you, Rubes. I'm so glad you're home." He pulls himself up onto the stool next to me.

"It's quiet in here tonight," I say, looking around. "And where are all the locals? I don't recognize any of the people here."

His face drops into a frown as he looks around. "No, most of these are transient workers who now work on the island. The locals have started to avoid this place on weekends. They are not snobs, but the workers aren't very friendly. Some of them are downright rude."

I take another sip of my drink and give him a nudge. "So, rumor has it you are in a committed relationship. Surely the great Joshua Woods has not actually found someone he can be happy with. What was it you used to say? Why put limits on your love when you had so much to share," I tease.

A goofy grin crosses his face, and a dreamy look appears in his eyes as he looks over my shoulder.

Turning on my stool, I see movement down by the wine bar. One of the most beautiful men I have ever seen walks around it. As he strides toward us, I note his lithe limbs are elegant and he moves like a predator stalking his prey. His dark hair is shaved on either side of his head, long on top, and stylishly pushed backward. His cheekbones are sharp enough to cut glass, and he has a smattering of stylish stubble across his jaw. When he reaches up to push his hair back, I can see his ears have a slight peak, giving away his elven heritage. Moving my eyes downwards, I admire his long, lean body that is covered by black leather pants and a black button-down shirt. His bright green eyes sparkle with delight, the only hint of color to be seen.

"Ruby, I think you have a little drool," Josh says, using a finger to close my mouth. He gets up and draws the fae into his arms, where he places a kiss on him that leaves me breathless. Damn! Bram was right, this man is breathtaking. "Hey, babe, come and meet my old friend," he says, drawing him onto his abandoned stool and wrapping his arms around him from behind.

"Ruby, this is Galan. Galan, this is Ruby." Josh gestures to me like a game show hostess. "Queen of candy and Regan's naughtier half."

I hold out my hand. "It's lovely to meet the person who finally got this guy to settle down. Goodness knows it hasn't happened before." Josh sends me a dirty look as Galan takes my hand and places a kiss on the back of it.

"Ruby," he says, his voice a musical delight to my ears. "I have heard so much about you and the Tempting Ten. I've been looking forward to meeting you."

I cringe at the name. "God, that name is awful! They can't possibly still be calling us that." Josh smirks at me. "So, tell me how you met this one," I ask curiously, gesturing to Josh.

A gentle smile crosses his face. "I met him when he came to the fae realm to inquire about selling fairy wine through the tavern."

I take a sip of my drink, finishing it off, and when Josh returns to the other side to make me another, he takes over the story.

"They told me of Galan and his family, and how they were the makers of the best wine in all of the fae realm, so I met with his family. It was instant attraction. I mean, look at him, who wouldn't be attracted? It turned out that Galen is the younger brother and won't inherit the business, so he decided to move here. We created a partnership and added onto the brewery. He makes our own brand of wine here with a mixture of earth and fairy grapes, giving us a product not available anywhere else." He looks proudly at his partner. "Not only is it hugely popular here, but it's also huge in the fae realm too."

I glance at Galan and find him squirming in his seat, looking very uncomfortable. I have a feeling there is more to the story, but as long as Josh is happy, why would I pry? "Well, I'm happy for you both."

We spend the next hour chatting about mutual friends. I also talk to Josh about getting me a few beer barrels to use as displays, which he is happy to do for me. The crowd has picked up, and although there still aren't a lot of familiar faces, it's enough for both Josh and Galen to have to serve, leaving me on my own. The alcohol is giving me a buzz, and I'm feeling no pain when I hear a commotion at the door. Regan and Maddock walk in, and they slide up to the bar and sit on either side of me, waving to Josh. He throws them a thumbs-up.

"Did you get things sorted with Josh?" Regan asks, surveying the tavern.

"Yep, all sorted, and with Bram starting work on

the shop tomorrow, it should all be good to go by the start of next week. My new candy line will be ready as well. I'll have to do some marketing and get some enthusiasm for the island again, and then I'm going to call Tats and demand she come home. In fact, I'm going to make all of the Tempting Ten come home if it's the last thing I do." I throw my fist into the air, and the guys stare at me with wide eyes.

"Whoa, Rubes, what are you drinking?" Regan reaches for my glass and takes a sniff.

"The panty dropper or panty snatcher or something. Watch out, Maddock." I throw a wink at him, and Regan's mouth falls open. I'm laughing so hard, I realize I need to pee. Jumping off my seat, I wander toward the restrooms, running my finger across Maddock's shoulders as I go. I just wanted to feel if he is as hard under his shirt as he looks. As I walk away, I turn back to see him watching me with hooded eyes. Blowing him a kiss, I push through the door with the hamster in a dress on it. I pee, wash my hands, and wander back out to the bar.

As I walk past the wine bar, I'm stopped by Galen. He puts a glass of sparkling, glittery pink wine into my hand, waving me off when I try to pay him. "Let me know what you think."

I take a sip, and a twinkling, shimmering feeling bubbles on my tongue and down my throat. I'm hit with feelings of lightness and joy. "Wow, this is amazing," I remark, and then I have an idea. "Can I get a couple of bottles of this to try in a new fudge recipe when the kitchen's running again? I think it would be amazing!"

"As long as I get to try it," he replies. "I'll send a couple of extra bottles with Regan's order for the manor."

"Awesome, thanks." I salute him with the champagne flute and continue back to the guys. Halfway back, I look up and discover a group of girls have surrounded Regan and Maddock. I recognize the twins, Jenna and Julie, as well as Sheree, the girl who left Lucille in the lurch. There are two more, a dark-haired girl who looks to be of Asian descent and another blonde, this one more dirty blonde than platinum. I watch as Sheree runs her finger up Maddock's arm, wearing a simpering smile and fluttering her eyelashes. Maddock looks super uncomfortable, and Regan is fending off the twins' advances. Well, that just pisses me off.

I saunter up to the group, pushing my way between Sheree and Maddock. Throwing myself into his lap and winding my arms around his neck, I place little kisses along his jawline. His hands come around and grab hold of my hips, stopping me from wiggling in his lap, but it's too late, I can feel the hardness developing underneath me. "I missed you so much. It was so kind of the girls to keep you company while I was away." I turn to Sheree. "Though I'm surprised you have the nerve to show your face, considering how rotten you were to his mother this morning," I finish, growling at her.

The girls gasp in shock, and Sheree gets a deadly look on her face. Grabbing me by the arm, she yanks me off Maddock's lap. "What do you think you are doing with my boyfriend?" She pushes me out of the way and snuggles up to him. I look at him in surprise, and he gets a sheepish look on his face before his eyes glaze over. I feel a wave of magic, but in my anger and shock, I can't get a clear read on where or who it came from. I look at Regan, who also has a shocked look on his face.

"What's going on, Maddock? I thought your mom told this girl that you were taken," Regan asks him.

"Mom always thought that Ruby and I should be together. Both she and Pru schemed and planned while she was away, but I'm afraid they are delusional."

A stab of hurt sears my chest at his comment, and I take an involuntary step back. Regan puts his hand on my waist to steady me. I look between Maddock and Sheree, the hurt evident on my face.

"Mind your own business, bitch. You don't know shit about this town. You've been gone too long. The Tempting Ten are history," she sneers. "And before you know it, this town will—" Julie elbows her violently in the side, and she cuts off abruptly.

The girls throw each other some looks, and the dirty blonde puts on a fake smile as she looks down the bar. "We need drinks. Where is the damn bartender?"

"Who knows, Minnie?" The Asian girl rolls her eyes. "Those two bartenders are probably sucking face out back. It's so gross. Why do we come to this bar?" she spits out.

Now that's the last straw. Regan and I both turn to the girl. "Listen, bitch, I don't know who the fuck you think you are, but that bartender is actually the owner, and you are not even good enough to breathe the same air as him. I suggest you take your skanky ass out of here and find somewhere else to socialize from now on."

"That man is our friend," Regan growls. "If you don't like his sexual orientation, you should probably leave and take your friends with you. We will not tolerate that kind of discrimination here."

I look at Maddock, expecting him to defend his friend as well, but he still has a vague expression on his face. Something is not right.

"Now, now, she really didn't mean it badly. She has no filter, sorry," Julie apologizes to Regan, ignoring me. She goes to put her hands on him, and I pull him away. She shoots me a death glare.

I turn to Regan. "I'm done for the night. The bar has suddenly become nauseating, can you take me home? I'll leave my car here and get it in the morning."

He nods and goes down to the end of the bar to

settle our tab and say goodbye to Josh. I eye the five women and Maddock warily. They have all taken seats at the bar and are whispering quietly to each other. Sheree has her hands all over Maddock, and he doesn't seem to be putting up a fight. I want to test him for that spell again, but I need to be closer to him.

Regan comes back over, and we leave. He shouts goodbye to Maddock but frowns when he gets no response. He puts his hand on my waist and guides me to the door. Pushing it open, we exit into the crisp night air.

"Do you know what's weird?" I murmur to him. "Supposedly all the young people have left town, and it looks like most are people between the age of eighteen and thirty, but you're still here. So are Maddock, Josh, and Bram. Can you think of any others?"

Regan stops with a look of surprise on his face. "Huh, you're right. There's also Taylor Crimson and Cullen Crowe, but he is out of town this week. The new mayor is a vamp, so he looks young, and of course there are Jandar and Galan, but elves age differently than us, so I'm not sure how old any of them are."

"If this is a spell that affects a particular age group, they won't be affected if they are older. It's something to look into. But why aren't you guys affected? There must be a reason. Also, what was all that in there?" I ask, gesturing back toward the bar.

Regan looks uncomfortable. "The Asian girl is Mia, and she has been dating Taylor. Sheree is obviously with Maddock, and Minnie has been trying to convince Cullen to date her."

"And Julie has been trying to catch your eye, but the twins keep cockblocking her. Gosh, I love those kids." I laugh at the look on his face. "So they have all been trying to date guys who are heavily involved in the town or part of the coven. I guess Galan and Josh are off-limits because they have each other."

He shrugs uncomfortably.

"Look, I need to tell you something. Maddock had a negativity spell on him this afternoon, and it was heavy and suffocating. I did a cleanse smudge, and it broke the spell, but I felt magic in there."

He nods his head in agreement.

"I think it's been redone. We need to find out if those girls are witches and which coven they are from. It's why I wouldn't let Julie touch you. You seem to be unaffected at the moment."

He looks apprehensive. "What are we going to do about Maddock? He needs that removed. His indifference to you is not how he really feels. I wouldn't have given you hope if it wasn't the case."

"I'm not sure, I'll have to talk to Mom about it. She may have some ideas."

We walk to his car and he drives me back to the

cottage. As he pulls up and puts the hand brake on, he turns to me and says, "Hang in there, Ruby, don't give up on Maddock just yet."

I just shrug my shoulders and give him a kiss on the cheek. I hop out and wave goodbye as he drives back to the manor, his tires kicking up dust on the road. I wait until the taillights disappear before I head inside to bed alone.

CHAPTER
Ten

Maddock

As I watch Ruby and Regan walk away, I feel nothing. She told me there was a spell on me this afternoon and removed it, or she said she did. After that, I felt almost normal again, and we had a moment. It felt good and right. But thinking about it now, how do I know that *she* didn't actually put a spell on me?

The girls are quietly talking to each other, and Sheree is perched in my lap. I've had a few beers, so I should feel something, anything, but it's like I'm numb inside. It's like I'm watching everything that is going on around me on a screen. I can see Josh and Galan having a conversation at the other end of the bar, frowning in my direction. I know I should feel something, but I just don't.

When Ruby was wiggling on my lap before, I felt a whole heap of something, but it was like a candle in the wind—there and then gone.

A cold breeze blows on the back of my neck, bringing me back to the present. Turning around to see where it came from, I see Cole and Taylor standing in the doorway, looking around. I wave my hand and gesture to the spare stools next to us. Smiling, they head our way. Jenna and Mia exchange whispers before turning and throwing themselves at the guys. Taylor gives Mia a kiss on the cheek, but Cole sidesteps Jenna and takes a seat next to me, waving at Josh as he does.

Joshua heads down the bar. "Cole, Sheriff." He nods to both of them. "What can I get you?"

Taylor's eyebrows rise in surprise. "Two drafts of the Hamster Golden Ale, thanks. What's with the formality, Josh? You've never been like this before."

"And you've never had such appalling taste in friends before, Taylor, even when you were hanging out with those moonshine making bear shifters when we were younger. At least they weren't bigoted bastards."

Taylor frowns as Josh walks away. He pours the two beers, places them in front of the guys, and walks away.

I'm guessing Galan's fae hearing must have

picked up what Mia said before and they have taken offense. Again, I can't bring myself to care. I watch as Sheree and the girls walk toward the bathrooms. Taylor turns to me with a raised eyebrow. "What was that about?" he asks curiously.

I shrug, disinterested. "Mia made a rude comment about Galen and Josh. Galen must have heard it with his fae ears."

Taylor looks surprised. "Really? She was rude?"

Cole scoffs, and Taylor scowls at him.

"What?" Taylor questions.

Cole shakes his head. "For a smart man, you really aren't paying attention. Is your nose not working? Every word out of those girls' mouths are half-truths. They smell of dark magic and wrongness. How can you not scent it? They smell of disgust every time Josh or Galen come close."

Taylor looks stunned. "No, I don't get any of that. They smell human to me."

Cole growls, "Well, I would get Pru to check you for spells then, because none of those girls are human." As I listen to their conversation, I should be showing some reaction, but again I feel numb.

"Did you know this?" Taylor asks me. "Why didn't you tell me?"

"Because I don't care," I reply to his accusations. "It's not like we have lots of options in this goddess forsaken town." That pit of despair inside me grows deeper.

He looks surprised. "But Ruby is back now, so you don't have to worry."

I finish the rest of my beer before placing it down on the bar and signaling for another. It will be my sixth, but who's counting, right? Josh frowns at me but goes ahead and pours it.

Turning to him, I say, "I wouldn't touch that untrustworthy bitch if my life depended on it." Josh places the beer in front of me. His, Cole's, and Taylor's mouths drop open in shock at my words.

"What is wrong with you?" Josh asks.

Before I can answer, the girls come back from their group trip to the bathroom. Grabbing Sheree, I pull her toward me and mash my lips to hers, and her tongue slides into my mouth. Maybe this will help them get the picture. Pulling my mouth away, I settle her on my lap and pick up my beer. Josh snorts in disgust and walks away. Taylor can't stop staring, but he absentmindedly wraps his arms around Mia, pulling her close. Jenna is trying to talk to Cole, but I can see he doesn't want anything to do with her. He gets up and walks down to the other end of the bar to talk to Galen and Josh.

Sheree starts to whisper dirty words into my ear. She suggests we head back to my place, and it sounds like a pretty good idea to me. Draining the last of my beer, I head down the bar to settle my tab. Josh swipes my card in judgmental silence, but I can't bring myself to give a fuck.

Waving goodbye to them all, I grab Sheree by the hand and drag her out to the parking lot. Realizing I don't have a car because I came with Regan, I look around for Sheree's, but then I remember she's not a townie, so no car. "Crap, I don't have my car."

Her smile drops in disappointment. She thinks for a moment, and then her face lights up with a suggestion. "Do you have keys to your mom's store?" I don't, but I can use magic to break in. This thought should disgust me, but it's not a bad idea. It's certainly warmer than fucking her against a tree.

"Let's go."

Wrapped around each other, we walk toward the ice cream store. It's slow going as we paw at each other. Before we can leave the parking lot, though, a set of lights flash in our eyes and a car stops directly in front of me.

Shielding my eyes, I break away from Sheree. "Fuck, turn the lights off," I grumble.

"Man, what the hell? Where were you going?" Regan demands as he steps out of the car.

"None of your business," Sheree snaps, grabbing my hand to drag me around the car.

"Maddock, I can't let you do this," Regan says as he approaches me, holding his hands up. "You look like you've had a few, and I don't want you to regret something in the morning. I wouldn't be your best friend if I didn't say anything."

I stop, swaying on my feet while I consider his words.

Sheree puts her hands on my arm and whines, "Are you going to let him speak like that?" A wave of raging anger flows through my body, and before I can do anything else, I pull back my fist and swing it at his face. He ducks, leaning to one side, and I stumble over. Turning around, I go to take another swing, and again, he dodges.

Sheree has run back to the Hamster, screaming, "Fight," and Regan just laughs at me now.

"What the fuck, man? Are you letting a little bitch get between us?" Furious at his words, I try to tackle him and have more success. We go tumbling to the ground, but he continues to laugh. My fists aren't coming anywhere near him, and I realize he has cast a counterspell. Using my own magic and the anger I feel, I conjure a knife. That wipes the laughter off his face quickly.

"Not laughing now, are you?" I slur at him, spit flying out. His look of disappointment is toxic. It spreads through me like wildfire. At the feeling, I let the knife dissipate. Cole and Taylor arrive, pulling us apart, with Josh and Galen not far behind them.

"Cut it out, Maddock. Regan, get him home before I throw him in jail for disturbing the peace!" Taylor orders Regan. All the fight has left my body. The disappointment on the face of a man who is like a brother to me was enough to break through the fury. What have I done?

Regan helps me to the passenger side of the car, opening the door for me. I grab him by the head, putting my forehead against his as tears spill from my eyes. "I'm so sorry, man. I don't know what happened."

He hugs me tight, clapping me on the back. "Don't worry, Mads, we will get it all figured out. Tomorrow's another day. Let's just get you home so you can sleep it off."

I sit in the car and he closes the door. Going around to the other side, he gets in and starts it up. Staring unfocused through the front window, I see a group of girls illuminated in the glare of the head-lights. Sheree is surrounded by the others, and the look of fury on her face is enough to rival the one that just left my body. I guess our plans did get ruined, but again, the numbness surrounds me, and I can't bring myself to care. Regan leaves the parking lot and heads for the manor. I guess I'm staying with him tonight.

CHAPTER
Eleven

Ruby

I wake up the next morning with a to-do list a mile long. I look up at the skylights in the roof, and I see the green of the trees outside, but they are indistinct and blurry. I wave my hand at the glass, and there's a flash of light before the window becomes transparent. The leaves on the giant oak trees that surround the cottage are rustling gently in the morning breeze, and a feeling of serenity and clarity fills my body.

Rolling out of bed, I head downstairs to my kitchen, the metal stairs cool under my feet. I wave my hand at the kettle, turning it on, as I go in search of my tablet. I find it on the coffee table where I plugged it into the wall to charge. Needing to write myself a list of all the things I have to do, I sit down at the counter.

The kettle starts to whistle, so I wave my hand at it again. A cupboard door opens and a cup flies out. A tea bag comes from another cupboard, soaring into the cup. The kettle then lifts up and fills the cup with hot water, then the tea bag jiggles up and down, turning the water dark. The kettle lowers down to the counter, and the cup floats up and toward me before gently setting down next to my tablet. A wisp of steam floats up toward the ceiling as I wave at the fridge, and then it opens and the milk floats out. It makes a wobbly path to the counter and sets down rather abruptly, teetering to one side. I snatch it with my hand before it can tip over. Hmmm, my magic muscles need a lot more work. Opening it up, I add it to my tea.

I take a sip, feeling the warmth sliding down my throat, soothing me and calming my erratic thoughts. Grabbing my tea and tablet, I wander out to the sunroom and throw myself on one of the couches. I lean back, holding my drink in one hand, and admire the view out of my sunroom windows.

With the cottage surrounded by trees on all sides, all that can be seen of the manor through the dense foliage is one of the spires at the top of a turret. It's why Regan and I used to like playing down here when we were little and visiting our grandparents. We loved the feeling of freedom, playing all kinds of games. As we got older, we'd have campfires and parties with our friends. Booze flowed, and the games got more mature, but through all the ups and downs, kisses, and fights, we all stayed friends.

Which brings me to thoughts of the Tempting Ten. Obviously the spell is *still* affecting them, since no one else has returned yet. I must speak to Mom about all the spells surrounding the island and influencing people, but first I need to talk to Tatiana. I snap my fingers and my phone lands in my lap. I put my cup of tea down and dial her number, waiting while I hear it ring, but it goes to voicemail.

"Tats! It's Rubes! You need to call me back as soon as you get this. Shit is happening, and I need you. Both your mom and Maddock are in trouble. Call me."

I press the button to disconnect, dropping the phone back in my lap and blowing out a breath in frustration. If that's not enough to put a rocket up her ass, I'm not sure what is.

My phone rings, making me jump in fright. Wow, that was quick, but when I look at the screen, I realize it's not Tatiana, but Bram. "Hey, Bram, what's up?"

"Hey, Ruby. Sorry to be calling so early, but you may want to come down to the store. I've just arrived to start work, but the front window has been smashed, and it looks like the shop has been trashed.

I've called the sheriff, but he may want to talk to you and your parents."

I jump up off the couch, and my stomach drops. I rush back into the house to grab my car keys with the phone shoved between my ear and shoulder. "Crap, okay. Have you called Mom and Dad?"

"No. Regan and Maddock are both here too, and Regan's on the phone at the moment."

"Okay, I'll get dressed and be right there. Don't let the sheriff go in until Mom and I arrive. There are some spells we can do to check for sabotage or for traps," I tell him in a rush.

"Yeah, okay, I'll let him know." He hangs up.

I race around, looking for clothes, when I stop abruptly. Seriously, when am I going to get used to using magic again? I snap both fingers, and the tank top and pajama shorts I was wearing disappear. Instead, I'm now wearing red capri pants and a white, fitted, scoop neck top and sneakers appear on my feet. Grabbing the keys off the bench and shoving my phone and tablet into my backpack, I run out the door, pulling it shut behind me. Looking around the empty front yard, I realize my car is not here. It's still parked at the Hamster. Damn it. Regan is in town already, and Mom and Dad are probably on their way.

Taking a deep breath, I try to calm my heart rate. My magic has slowly trickled back into my body since I came home and was released from that spell, but I still haven't tried to teleport yet. Clearing my mind and soaking up the energy of nature, I visualize the front of the shop and clap my hands together. There's a flash of light, then absolute darkness. When I reappear into the light, I'm directly in front of my shop. Dropping to the ground, dizzy and disoriented, I try desperately to hold the vomit inside when a wave of pain hits me.

I can hear voices, but I'm still disoriented, and I can't tell who's talking to me. Unknown hands help me stand up, then arms lift me before carrying me. I'm placed down on the wooden bench a little farther down the street, and my head is pushed between my legs as a hand rubs up and down my back. My breath saws in and out as I try to control it.

"Deep breaths, Rubes, deep breaths," I hear Regan murmur as my hearing returns to me.

"What were you thinking?" a voice screeches at me, and I silently wish my hearing hadn't returned. I slowly sit up, and my mother glares at me with murder in her eyes. I guess she's going to finish what the teleportation started.

I roll my eyes at her.

"Don't you roll your eyes at me, young lady. You are not too old to have your bottom paddled." Ha, she always threatens that but has never done it. "You haven't used your magic regularly for years, and you think you're ready to teleport? It's like a muscle, Ruby. If you don't use it, it weakens. For goddess's sake, what you just did was the equivalent of a fat man attempting to run the hundred-meter sprint. It's amazing you didn't suffer a stroke."

My breathing has finally slowed, and I start to reply, but she holds her hand up.

"No, I don't want to hear it. It was reckless and stupid. Don't do it again until you've had more practice. I don't care if you are the strongest teleporter we have."

"I'm sorry, Mom, you are right."

An expression of shock crosses her face, and she looks at Regan. "Did you hear that?"

He nods with a smirk.

A look of triumph crosses her face, and she does a little victory dance in the street. I ignore her gloating and turn to look back toward the shop. "What happened? Have you checked for spells or a clue to who did this? What about the security cameras?" Still feeling unsteady, the words rush out.

From where I am sitting with Mom and Regan, I can see Dad, Bram, Maddock, and the sheriff all standing in front of the shop. My spirits drop when I realize Maddock wasn't the least bit concerned about me. He was always the first to help me when we were kids and I hurt myself. Regan pats me on the knee and draws my attention back to him. The look on his face is worrying me.

"Taylor only just got here, so we are not sure. He was over at the Hamster. I'm sorry, Rubes, but someone has slashed all the tires on your car and smashed the windows. It looks like someone has it out for you."

"Your dad looked at the video surveillance from his phone, but it's blank. It's been switched off, so it shows us nothing. If you are still not feeling up to it, I'll get the boys to help with the spell to check for residue and traps," Mom says.

I shake my head. "I'm alright, just give me a few more minutes, please." Regan gets up and walks over to the others, leaving Mom and me. The town is still relatively quiet at this time of morning. I can hear the sound of horse hooves and carriage wheels somewhere along the street, and I watch as a few people go in and out of Buttered Biscuit for their morning coffee. I snap my fingers, and a couple of takeaway cups appear in my hands.

I smile as I pass one to Mom. "Don't worry, it's all coming back to me. I just forget to use it."

She smiles and takes a cup. "Make sure to leave some money on the bench for Beatrix."

I nod. "Already taken care of."

I continue to watch while I recover my bearings and breath. A small crowd has gathered, watching what is going on around the store. I recognize a few of the locals, but most are unfamiliar to me. I turn to my mom and lower my voice to make eavesdropping difficult.

"Mom, while we are sitting here, can we do a

discovery spell? I have a funny feeling that the spell on us was not the only one. Yesterday I found one on Maddock. It's suffocating the light out of him. I fixed it, but when we were at the Hamster yesterday, it was replaced. Have a look at his aura, it's muddy and writhing with negativity."

She looks up, her lips pursed in thought as she focuses on Maddock. Her forehead creases in a frown as she nods her head and grabs hold of my hand. Discreetly, she sends out a searching spell, and what comes back to us is shocking. Both of us gasp at the backlash.

"Holy crap! Mom, there is so much wrong with this town. I count three."

She nods her head in agreement. "There seem to be two circling the island. One repels humans, the other supes. The third one seems to be embedded in the town. That one is encouraging young people to leave the island. I can feel the negativity, and it's like a fog. I don't know how I didn't notice before, but there is some very dark magic at work."

"Don't blame yourself, Mom. It was probably spelled in layers and you didn't notice because it was done over time. The other thing I noticed is the older female coven girls were chased off, but most of the boys are still here. There are so many questions, and we have very little in the way of answers. We need to do more."

Mom's nodding her head, her red curls bobbing

with the action. "It will take some powerful spells to remove the ones from the island. We will need more of the girls back before we attempt that. But we should be able to deal with Maddock's spell today. Let's handle the shop, and then we will figure out how to deal with Maddock. We will need to get him away from that Klingon." She nods toward Maddock.

We both watch as Sheree walks out of the group of people who had been watching all the commotion. She strolls up to him, drapes her arms around his neck, and pulls him into a deep kiss, interrupting the conversation he was involved in. I watch as his mother tries to get his attention from the doorway of her shop. Both Mom and I gasp in shock as he ignores her and grabs Sheree by the hand before they wander off in the direction of the blacksmith, ignoring both his mother and the guys standing around the store. We watch as Lucille wrings her hands together and turns to go back into her shop, the light catching on the tear sliding down one cheek.

"Motherfucker!" my mom whispers under her breath. I turn to look at her, my eyes wide in shock as a snort escapes the side of my mouth. "Right," she says, standing up and reaching down to help me. "We're wasting time. Let's get on with it."

We walk over to the shop to hear the end of what Sheriff Crimson is saying to Dad. "And unfortunately, we have no other leads. It's like the area has been magically cleansed."

Dad reaches out and shakes his hand. "Thanks, Taylor, for letting us know." He turns to us. "Taylor says all the surveillance cameras in the areas were wiped for a period of half an hour last night, and he can't get any trace of a scent. There was a really thick fog that rolled in late last night, keeping people inside, and those who were around didn't see or hear anything."

"Do you think you can try a spell on the store and see if you can get anything, Pru?" Taylor asks my mom.

She smiles at him and nods her head, and a look of determination crosses her face. "Nobody messes with my town and my friends and gets away with it. Time to pull out the big guns."

She pulls me over until we are standing in front of the smashed window. I stand on my tiptoes and peer inside over the broken glass, and my heart sinks to the bottom of my stomach. The store is in ruins. The displays have been trashed, candy is strewn from one end of the shop to the other, and ants crawl everywhere throughout the store. From what I can see, nothing is salvageable. We need to get in there to be sure, but first, we need to check for booby traps and spell residuals from the caster—if there are any.

We clasp hands, and as she starts to murmur the spell under her breath, I channel power into her to boost the spell. She finishes casting it, and a flash of light illuminates the inside of the candy store. Traps or attack spells would show up as crimson patches of light, but this is all clear. Just as the spell dissipates, I feel the caster's residual magic. It is the same as the one I touched on Maddock yesterday. I turn and look at Mom, but she just shakes her head in response. The light fades, and we give the sheriff the all clear to go inside. He shoves open the door, which is made difficult by the debris blocking the entrance.

"Whoever did this must have broken the window first and then teleported into the shop, as there is no way they could have climbed through that jagged glass without cutting themselves. They also blocked the door with all the debris," I say, pointing out the window and the trouble with the door.

Taylor grunts in agreement and starts to sniff around the store, literally. We all stand still while he assesses the smells, but his frown and the shake of his head tells me everything I need to know. "Sorry, Ruby. I just can't pick up anything amongst the smell of the sugar. All this crushed candy and the different flavors are muddling everything up. Nothing stands out."

I'm really not surprised. I can tell just by looking that nothing can be saved. All the products are damaged beyond salvation. I look into the kitchen to find that the bags of sugar have been slashed, the colorings were emptied over the sugar, creating a rainbow mess, and the flavorings were poured out over the floor. The machines have been smashed beyond repair as well. I can tell the arms of the candy puller were used to break the display cabinets. A shiver of despair covers my body, and I wrap my arms around my waist, hugging myself. "Not your fault, Sheriff, but thanks anyway."

"I'll continue to ask around to see if anyone saw anything, but I wouldn't get your hopes up. If you come across the caster, you make sure you let me know. And, Rubes, I'm off tomorrow if you need help cleaning up."

"Thanks, Taylor, I appreciate it."

He walks out, leaving Mom, Dad, Bram, and Regan to survey the damage.

"Oh well, nothing to be done for it now. Luckily we were redoing the store anyway," Dad comments, trying to be positive.

"I would have liked to have kept the inventory. Do you know how busy I'll be trying to restock this place? You know I love making candy, but I don't think I will be sleeping any time soon," I complain.

Mom just waves her hand and the store instantly empties. All the mess, broken glass, trashed candy, and ants are gone, and a blank shell, empty and barren, is left behind. "There, fixed. Now it's a fresh, clean slate for Bram to work with and less work for us. Honey, you know we will help as much as we can," she says, her voice echoing through the empty shop. Putting her arm around my shoulders, she starts to issue orders like a drill sergeant. "Bram, you and Gerald have the store, yes?" He nods at her. "Regan, you go back to the manor, I know you're busy. Alastair, you go with him and help with what he needs. Ruby and I will head back to her place and write a list of everything we need to make and start on the inventory. We may need to make a trip to Toronto to get supplies since we have lost everything. Maddock can take you, since we are all busy and he has some amends to make," she says, turning to me.

I snort in disgust. "I can't even get him to look at me, Mom, even when I just about spliced myself when teleporting. What makes you think I can get him to take me shopping?"

"I will make it a coven decree. He will have to do it. Before you go, we will make a protection potion for him which will make it impossible to drape the negativity spell over him again. You can add it to a drink and give it to him on your trip. We will anchor it with a drop of your blood, Ruby."

Regan snorts. "Sounds a bit like a love spell, Mom. I know Maddock is into Ruby, but don't take away his free will."

"No, nothing like that," she argues. "This will allow Ruby to feel if he is tampered with at any stage, but the potion itself is strong and should protect him permanently. We may need to get it into every one of the townspeople so that individuals cannot be messed with. I will talk to the mayor and see if I can have it added to the town water supplies, which may be the easiest way. It will protect the residents and any of the tourists visiting the town against negative influences."

My spirits start to brighten now that we have some plans being put into place. We all agree with our orders, and Dad and Regan head off to the manor as Gerald walks through the door of the store to help Bram with the renovations.

"Hello, Ruby, Pru," he greets, nodding to us both. "I hear you have had some bad luck, but on the bright side, we can get going with the new stuff now." He gestures to the picnic basket he carried with him. "Beatrix sent plenty of food along to keep up our strength, so it shouldn't be more than a couple of days before we can get the store up and running again." He winks at us, and a weight lifts off my chest.

The store is in good hands, so we tell them goodbye and Mom and I stroll outside to her car.

CHAPTER
Twelve

Ruby

Before heading back to my place, I ask Mom to drive me to the Hamster. When we arrive in the parking lot, there is no sign of the Mustang. I ask Mom to wait while I go inside to see if Josh knows what happened.

When I try the front doors to the bar, they are shut tight, and the sign next to the door with the hours reminds me how early it still is. I wander around the side of the building, and I hear clanging sounds, so I stroll in that direction. Rounding the corner, I find a lovely sight.

Both Josh and Galan are shirtless, rolling empty kegs from the back door of the pub into the brewery facility. Standing back, I admire the glistening, rippling muscles for five minutes. After my morning, I deserve a little sugar. One of the kegs bangs against another, creating a loud ringing sound and knocking me out of my daze.

"Hi, guys," I shout above the noise. They both stop what they are doing and look up. "Why are you doing manual labor when you could snap your fingers and move them?"

"Because, sweet Ruby," Josh says, wrapping his arms around me and smacking a kiss to my forehead.

I push him away. "Gross, you're all sweaty."

"How would we look this good without the manual labor?" He flexes his arms, making body-builder poses.

Galan scoffs. "Speak for yourself, I don't have to work for anything."

Josh grabs him and pulls him close, giving him a gentle kiss on the lips before whispering, "No, you do not."

My heart wistfully skips a beat. I notice they both have a matching mark. Galan's is over his chest, whereas Josh's is on his shoulder blade. "What's that mark?" I ask, pointing at Galan's chest.

He looks down, smiling. "That's my mate mark. Elves have predestined mates. The mark shows up on both people's bodies when they first come in contact with each other. It burns so you don't miss it happening. Best five minutes of pain in my life."

They give each other smoldering glances. I'm so jealous.

"Okay, settle down, you two," I joke awkwardly. "I just want to know if you've seen my car, and then you can go back to ogling each other."

They snap out of it. "Shit, your car, Ruby! We are so sorry," Josh apologizes. "Nothing like that has ever happened before."

"No! People leave their cars here all the time, it's always been safe," Galan chimes in, "and we have cameras, but they show nothing." His accent gets stronger with his anger. "We had it towed for you and we will have it repaired as an apology. No, don't argue." He can see me opening my mouth to do just that. "And when we find out who did it, they will pay." Even half naked, he looks every bit the elven warrior.

Josh sees me eyeing his mate and sends me a wink. I mouth, "Lucky boy," to him before saying, "Thanks, guys. I'm only guessing, but this and the shop must be connected."

They nod their heads. "Taylor told us about the shop when we called to report the car. Is there anything we can do?" Josh asks.

"No, I think everything is under control. Listen, Mom's waiting in the car so I have to go. Thanks again."

"Say hi to Pru for us," Josh says, and I turn to leave, waving goodbye.

I'm relieved that's one less thing I have to worry about, but it means I'm going to be stuck without wheels, and my teleporting needs work—another reason to get my act together and practice more magic.

We spend the rest of the morning writing an inventory list for everything I need for the candy store and discussing the fate of the island. By late afternoon, we have a plan. Mom's busy in the kitchen, googling supply stores in Toronto, while I step out onto the back porch of the cottage. The steam drifting off the hot tub is inviting, and the thought of soaking in hot water after the day I've had is tempting, but first, I try to call Tatiana. Again, it rings before going to voicemail. I leave another message and hang up, stomping my foot in frustration. *Damn it, Tatiana, where are you?*

I hear a door bang behind me, so I walk back inside. Regan and Mom are in the kitchen with their heads together, whispering. I can just smell the scheming wafting in the air. They both look up as I enter, and the conversation stops.

"What's going on in here?" I ask them suspiciously, and their faces become very blank.

Mom gets up and walks around to fill up the kettle, turning on the tap. "I've ordered the machinery. It will be flown up in a couple of days, but you need to go to Toronto to pick up the colors and flavorings you need as well as the other bits and bobs. Oh, and sugar—lots of sugar. We also need to talk about our branding and redesigning our website, but we can do that later."

Regan comes to me with a severe expression. "Please help my friend, Ruby. I know he has been unbearable, but you know that's not him. His light is being smothered. Please help before it's too late." With that, he kisses my cheek and helps Mom up from her chair.

She grabs her handbag and walks to the front door with Regan moving quickly behind her. "Oh, and Maddock will pick you up tomorrow morning to drive you to Toronto and help you with all the bags of sugar." They both disappear out the door, leaving me standing here in bewilderment. "Oh, and the spell you need is written on the bench. Brew it tonight and put it in his morning coffee or something. Don't forget the drop of blood, Ruby." Mom's voice trails off as they get farther away.

I turn and see a pink Post-it Note lying next to my laptop. A breath huffs out as I sit down on the seat. I guess we are doing this then. Reading through the ingredients of the spell, I realize I need some supplies, so I call Happy Herbs, the local apothecary run by the Crowe family. They are also members of the Arbor Vitae Coven and have been supplying herbs and other items to the witch community for years. Placing an order that will be ready for me in thirty minutes, or so I'm promised, I thank Minerva and hang up.

While I'm waiting, I decide to test the hot tub on the deck. After locking the front door, I strip off my clothes and walk out onto the deck naked. I climb into the spa, the hot, steamy water easing the ache from my tired, tense muscles. I snap my fingers, and a glass of sparkling pink champagne appears on the edge of the hot tub. Now that's a great way to practice my magic. Leaning back, I allow my troubled thoughts to float away.

A little longer than thirty minutes later, and after more than one glass of champagne, I conjure up a towel, dry myself off, and walk back into the kitchen with it wrapped around me. Sitting on the kitchen counter are all the things I ordered from Happy Herbs. Rereading my mom's note, I roll my eyes. Of course she wants me to perform this naked. The woman is such a freaking hippy. Good thing I've had some champagne. Taking the ingredients, candles, an amulet, and a container to put the potion in, I head outside to the ceremonial clearing the coven often uses in the woods behind the manor.

Dropping my towel, I light both a white and pink candle, passing the amulet through the flames of the white one first. "To protect thee from harm," I chant, before passing the amulet through the flames of the pink candle and saying, "To protect thee from stress." I swing it back to the white candle. "To protect thee from negative influences."

I place the amulet into the cauldron in the center of the clearing and snap my fingers to light a fire underneath it. Pouring in some water, I add basil, bay leaves, oregano, peppermint, sage, and black pepper. It starts to boil furiously. Using the athame Maddock made me for my eighteenth birthday, I go to prick my finger, but a howl sounds out across the clearing, startling me, and I slice my thumb pad open, gushing blood into the cauldron. *Oops.*

Looking down at the potion, I see it has turned a vibrant pink color. Shrugging my shoulders, I continue on. Mom did say the blood was only so I would know if someone interfered with him again. I guess I will be extra tuned in.

"The Wiccan Law ye must obey. With pure love and faith, the Wiccan Creed to fulfill, shall harm none where you will. Impure act or inkling fold back on thee three by three. In Maddock's hold now ye be, nary a thought of impurity. For any thought or speech of hate, forever become your fate. As you do unto thee, as I will, so mote it be."

When I finish the spell with ritual words, the fire flares, the water bubbles, and a wave of magic flows through me, caressing me with warm tingles before dissipating. Watching the flame die out, I magic some clothes onto my body.

Using a pair of tongs, I pull the amulet out of the water, string it on a cord, and then put it in my pocket to give to Maddock. I look into the cauldron, seeing a dark brown, tea-like liquid sitting in the bottom. I magic it up and out of the pot, the fluid flowing like a ribbon through the air to pour into the flask. I'll add some honey and lemon to it and tell him it's a pick-me-up tomorrow.

I then wrap all the items in my bath towel and conjure some water to ensure the fire is out before heading back to my cottage and my bed, praying to the goddess that all goes well.

That night, my dreams are haunted by visions of the Tempting Ten. The girls fade away, ceasing to exist. Skeletons cackle and dark spirits infect the island, and we are trapped, unable to escape, and powerless to change anything. Just as the island is about to be swallowed whole by a thorn encrusted vine, suffocating all life, I bolt upright in bed, breathing heavily with sweat covering my body.

What was that? A foreshadowing? Is that what will happen to the island?

Moving to the bathroom, I splash some water on my face, trying to clear the lingering creepy feeling the dream left me with. I stare at myself in the mirror, noting I look a little worse for wear. My pink hair is sticking out at all angles, and the red roots are very noticeable now. I need to use some magic to fix that. My green eyes are sunken and surrounded by dark circles, and even the freckles across my cheeks look pale and listless. Running my hand through my hair, I turn around and go back to bed. I climb in and pull the blankets up, but a sound on my window makes me jump. Looking up, I see a tree branch scraping across the glass. Jesus, that dream made me jumpy.

Rolling over and pulling the blanket over my ears to block out the noise, I settle in, but a movement at the end of my bed has me screaming and throwing back the covers. A knife instantly appears in my hand as I look around, but I can't see anything. A plaintive meow from the end of the bed has me looking over the edge. My quilt is writhing, and the meows are turning into hissing, screeching yowls. I climb off the mattress and untangle the heap.

"Holy hell, Sugar, you scared the crap out of me! Weird dreams and scratchy branches have made me nervous." Putting the quilt back on the bed, I pick Sugar up, give her a kiss, and place her down before hopping back into bed. She gives me a look of disdain, turns her back to me, and curls up on the end of the mattress.

I know she has forgiven me when her quiet purr sounds out across the room. Slowing my breathing down, I think about tomorrow and pray to the goddess Mom's spell works and we can fix Maddock. I'm not sure what we are going to do if we can't— what *I'm* going to do if we can't.

CHAPTER
Thirteen

Ruby

It's a struggle to get out of bed the next morning. Weird dreams plagued my sleep, so everything happens at a slower pace, but I'm still ready on time, with coffees in hand, when Maddock's black truck pulls up in front of the cottage. I go around to the passenger side and climb in. Shooting Maddock a smile, I pass him his special brew.

"Made you a pick-me-up drink. You've been looking a bit gray the last few times I've seen you." He grunts but grabs it and takes a large gulp. I let out a massive sigh of relief. Things should return to normal any minute now. I watch him closely as he puts the car into gear, but nothing changes. I'll give it a chance to work. Settling back in the seat, I watch as we pass the manor and head toward the docks. "Thanks so much for coming with me. I really need to get started on replacing all the candy, and I need the sugar like yesterday. I can't wait for the supply boat to come in."

He grunts before grumbling, "Pru and Mom didn't give me much of a choice."

I roll my eyes. Jesus, I hope that potion kicks in soon, or it's going to be a long-ass drive. Pulling my list out of my backpack, I study it. "I have a list of places to visit and supplies I need, but I'm not sure if we are going to be able to do this in one day." Looking up, I notice he has stopped at Buttered Biscuit. "What are we doing? Are you getting breakfast?" I ask, but he doesn't answer me.

He gets out, slamming the door behind him, and goes into the cafe. Climbing out, I follow him. This is getting annoying. If I thought my magic could handle the strain, I would just teleport myself there and then teleport the supplies home, but I don't think I could cope with that much yet.

The smells that greet my nose as I enter Buttered Biscuit are enough to make angels weep, and suddenly I'm not so annoyed at Maddock. Approaching the counter, I view the assortment of tasty treats, trying to decide what to choose.

"Morning, Ruby," Beatrix says with a smile,

wiping her hands on a dishcloth and putting it to the side. "What can I get you?"

"Beatrix, how can I decide when you have so many options?" I complain.

She laughs before replying, "Are you off to Toronto today for supplies?"

"Yes," I answer. "As soon as Maddock finishes whatever he is doing."

A frown crosses her face, and her eyes move to the seating area to the side. A peal of laughter can be heard, and I turn to look at what she's frowning at. Seated in a corner booth, which is why I didn't notice when I walked in, is Sheree. She is laughing at whatever Maddock is whispering in her ear. *Fuck!* My head bangs against the display case, and Beatrix snorts. Why can't I catch a break?

"Beatrix, I'm going to need your biggest pastry. One where I can't fit my foot in my mouth at the same time." She opens the cabinet and puts a few cakes in a box. Maddock and Sheree leave the booth and approach me holding hands.

"Hurry up, Ruby, we have a lot of driving to do. We'll be in the car."

"Both of you?" I question. I wince at my tone, but now I think I will probably need more than just sugar to get through this trip. I may have to conjure alcohol, depending on what the next words out of his mouth are. I mean, it's not like I can conjure up a gun and kill them both.

"Sheree's tagging along to keep me company," he replies then drags her through the door to the car.

"Because I'm chopped liver," I grumble quietly.

Beatrix smiles sympathetically and opens the warming cabinet. "Sugar just isn't going to cut it today, is it, love?" She piles a couple of greasy ham and cheese Danish into another bag. "Just eat yourself into a food coma and nap the whole way."

"It's about four hours, Beatrix," I whine. "I don't think I can handle it." Handing her my money, I grab my food and trudge back to the truck, stopping abruptly when I see Sheree has taken my front seat. *Fuck!* I kick a stone on the footpath. As I climb in, I notice my backpack and its contents are strewn across the floor in the back. "Bitch!" I mumble quietly under my breath.

"Sorry, Ruby, did you say something?" Maddock asks.

"I said I have an itch." I scratch my eye with my middle finger as he watches me in the rearview mirror. I duck my head and start picking up my stuff. The amulet from yesterday's spell has fallen out, and I shove it into my pocket, hoping I can place it on him at some point through the trip. Once I'm done, I sit up and strap in. Maddock starts the truck and heads toward the ferry.

After we board the ferry, I take my food and leave the truck, heading toward a peaceful seating area at the front so I don't have to spend any more time in the vehicle. I nod to a crewman as I walk past.

"You might want to check on those two. I'm not sure if he applied the parking brake because he's so distracted, if you know what I mean." I wink at him.

A slimy smile crosses his face, and he nods his thanks before heading back toward the truck. Laughing at my deviousness, I continue to the bow of the boat. Fresh air, coffee, and some pastries should lighten my mood immensely.

The ferry trip is nauseating, and that's not from me being seasick. By the time the truck hits solid ground and starts the almost three-hour drive to Toronto, I have already had enough. Once we all got back into the truck to drive it off the ferry, Sheree slowly inched farther and farther over on the bench seat until she was practically sitting in his lap.

The potion shows no sign of being effective. Maddock has barely said two words to me, and everything out of Sheree's mouth that's aimed in my direction is passive aggressive. It's excruciating. I discreetly conjure a blanket and wrap myself into a sad little cocoon. I don't really care if Sheree sees it and asks, I'll just tell her it was back here on the floor.

A tear rolls down my face at the thought of having lost Maddock permanently. I conjure a bottle of wine into my hand. Did someone order a pity party for one? Unscrewing the top, I take a swig and pull out my phone to text my mom.

Me: It didn't work!!!

Me: Sheree is here!!!

Mom: What do you mean it didn't work? That spell was flawless.

Mom: What did you do?

Me: Well, it didn't.

Mom: Did you seal it with a kiss?

Me: SMH WTF!

Mom: Language!

Me: You didn't say it had to be sealed with a kiss.

Me: How am I going to do that?

Mom: Well, when a boy likes a girl…

Me: Shut up, Sheree is here.

Mom: Oh yeah, that may be hard.

Mom: You'll work it out.

Me: *Middle finger*

Mom: *Smiley face*

The sound of giggling and a zipper being opened reaches me as I throw my phone on the floor of the truck. I hear Maddock whisper, "Not here, baby," and the zipper goes back up. Thank fuck for small miracles.

I settle down to make this wine my bitch, hoping and praying for sleep to put me out of my misery.

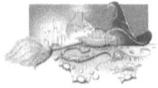

The sound of a door slamming wakes me from my dream of caramels, taffy, peanut butter cups, and hard candies. Stretching and sitting up, I wipe the drool away from the corner of my mouth and rub the sleep out of my eyes. Looking out the window, I see a large industrial building. I unstrap my seatbelt and climb out of the car with a frown, raising my arms high to stretch out the last of the kinks. Looking around in frustration, I see Maddock and Sheree strolling down a white sandy beach dotted with striped umbrellas. We're at Sugar Beach Park. What the hell?

Chasing after them, I shout, "Hey, what are you doing?" They ignore me and continue to the wall where the water meets the beach. There aren't many people around due to the cooling, fall temperature, but a few people are sitting on the lounge chairs here and there.

Breathing heavily from running through the sand, I finally reach them, placing my hands on my hips as I catch my breath before asking again. "Hey, I asked what you are doing." They turn toward me. Sheree has a frown on her face again. God, I think it's her default face.

"Sheree wanted to stretch her legs. I thought this would be a romantic place to do it," Maddock says, gesturing to the beach.

I look at him in surprise. "Who are you? It's like I don't even know you anymore."

"You don't," she snaps. "It would be sweet if it weren't for the third wheel." She simpers, snuggling into him.

"Third wheel? Third wheel?" I repeat, my voice getting louder. My blood rushes through my ears as my anger rises.

"Yes, third wheel," she snarls at me. "You really are getting in the way." Turning to Maddock, she pouts. "Tell her to go away."

"Go away?" That's it, my temper hits its breaking point. "Right, bitch, this is my trip you are hijacking. Maddock is here to help me out, not to take you on a date. I've got ingredients I need to buy and equipment to source. I don't have time for the two of you to be taking side trips. We need to get this done so I can return and replace all the stock that got damaged in the break-in." I turn to Maddock. "Please, I know you don't really like me at the moment, but this needs to be done, even if it's for Mom and Dad. Please, Maddock, tell her," I beg him.

She drops his arm and walks toward me. The dazed look stays on his face, and he seems to be oblivious. "Listen up, you little witch." She stalks toward me, and I take a couple of steps back. "Get it through your head, Maddock is mine now. That boat has sailed, and you need to let it go. If I want a romantic stroll, I get one. If I want to waste a whole day doing whatever, I will. And if I want to make it as difficult as possible for you, you are going to wish you never left Morbank Island." I look at him, but he still isn't paying too much attention to us. It's like the lights are on and nobody is home.

"What have you done to him?" I hiss at her. "What are you?"

A panicked look crosses her face briefly before it turns calculating. "Your worst nightmare. Too bad you're not going to be around to find out," she replies and shoves me hard in the chest with both hands. Stumbling backward in the sand, I lose my balance when I feel the fence hit the back of my knees. Before I can right myself, I'm tumbling over. My head cracks hard against the concrete, making me see stars, and my body continues to roll with an unseen force until I leave solid ground and plunge down into the freezing cold water. My muscles seize up, and everything is blurry and fuzzy as I sink lower and lower, unable to even panic, until there's nothing.

CHAPTER
Fourteen

Maddock

"Hey! Hey, help her! Someone help her!"

A voice behind me shakes me out of my daze. What was that? Turning around, I see a man and woman running toward us down the beach, pointing at something in the water. Spinning quickly, I look to where he's gesturing. Sheree is standing by the wall's edge, and there's no sign of Ruby.

"Quick," the man urges anxiously. "She hit her head when she fell in. She's been down there for a while."

I rush to where Sheree is. She's just standing there

watching. When I get close, she grabs my arm and a wave of disinterest flows through my body. I stop, watching the air bubbles float to the surface of the water.

The couple reaches us, their continuous, frantic cries penetrating my indifferent state, encouraging me to take action.

"What happened?" I ask Sheree as I strip off my shirt and shoes and climb over the little wire fence.

"She tripped and fell backward," Sheree replies, gesturing at the fence. "I tried to catch her, but I wasn't fast enough." The couple scoffs, and they shake their heads in disagreement, but I don't wait to hear what they have to say. Mumbling a temperature spell under my breath, I dive into the cold, deep water. It surrounds me in darkness, the chill held off by my enchantment. Needing to see, I hold out my hand and recite a spell in my head for light. A beam of light shines from my palm, illuminating the murky depths as I swim down in the direction the bubbles are coming from.

As I search, an amulet floats up out of the darkness. Shooting forward, I grab it, thinking Ruby must have dropped it, and tuck it into my pocket. The fog in my mind clears. Shit, Ruby! I frantically search the depths.

Catching a flash of light out of the corner of my eye, I turn quickly in that direction. There, floating in front of me like a siren in the sea with her pink hair streaming out behind her, is my Ruby. Kicking furiously, I swim toward her, snatching her before she can drift away. I drag her body behind me as I swim up, my lungs straining with the need for air. I break the surface and suck air into my deprived lungs. Grabbing Ruby around her chest, I tow her toward the wall where the couple stands, waiting to help pull her in.

Sheree is still standing on the other side of the fence with her arms crossed. I shake my head at the sight of her. Lifting Ruby up into the arms of the concerned couple, I use a quick spell to boost me up and out while they are distracted. They lay Ruby down on the concrete, and I move them out of the way. Kneeling down, I lean over Ruby, listening for breath and checking for a pulse. I find neither. My heart is pounding, and with shaking hands, I grab her nose and mouth, tip back her head, and give her two quick breaths. Then, using both hands, I thrust down on her chest, hoping to get her heart moving.

"Come on, Ruby, breathe!" I grunt as I do compressions.

The couple has climbed back over and are arguing with Sheree over something. Sheree grabs the man by the arm he is gesturing with and starts arguing back. I'm not going to worry about that, but hopefully he won't get violent. While they are distracted, I send a pulse of electricity through my hands and into her chest in the hope it will start her heart. Her whole body jolts, rising off the ground before falling down. I give her a couple more breaths and then recheck her pulse. This time, I can feel the pulse, but she's still not breathing, so I lean down and give her a couple more lifesaving breaths. After the second one, a pulse of power thrums through my body, sparking to life before dissipating. Shaking my head, I go to give her one more breath, but she starts to cough and splutter. Water flows from her mouth, so I roll her over and rub her back as she expels all the lake water she inhaled. Eventually, she stops, and I roll her toward me, wiping her mouth with the back of my hand and pushing her hair out of her face. She looks up at me, her skin pale and eyes wide.

"What happened?" she asks, her body shaking from the cold. I pull her up and circle my arms around her. My body heat spell is still working, so I'm able to keep us both warm.

"I'm not sure," I reply, looking back over at the others. They are no longer arguing, and the other couple has turned and walked away. That's strange, I would have thought they would have stayed to see if Ruby was alright before leaving. They were so concerned about her before.

Helping Ruby to her feet, I steady her as we climb over the fence. When we get to my clothes, I grab my shirt, shake out the sand, and hold it out to her. "Here, put this on." She goes to argue, but I step closer to her and whisper, "You can't conjure anything because I'm not sure if she knows we're witches or not, and I'm not prepared to share it."

"What are you whispering?" Sheree whines.

I take a step back and shake my head at her. "Nothing, just trying to convince Ruby to change her shirt until we can get back to the car." Her lips are blue, and her teeth are chattering furiously. "I'll turn around, just switch shirts."

She grabs it out of my hand, and I turn my back. Sheree approaches and puts her hands on me. A static shock hits me and bounces back onto her. She glances up in surprise, and a look of fury crosses her face as she glares over my shoulder at Ruby, but it quickly clears and she starts to rub her hands over my body.

"Oh, baby, you must be so cold, let me warm you up," she coos.

I shake her hands off in disgust. "Seriously? Ruby almost drowned, and that's all you can think about?"

Turning around, I see she has swapped out her shirt for mine. A wave of possession courses through my body when I see her dressed in my shirt. Wrapping my arms around her, I start the walk back to the truck.

"But... But... What about our walk?" Sheree complains.

"Fuck," I mumble under my breath. "What was I thinking, dating her?"

"S-s-s-spell," Ruby stammers.

I stop abruptly, turning her in my arms. "What did you say?" I demand. She looks shocked at the anger in my voice, and her eyes widen. She continues to shudder with the cold, but she shakes her head at me.

"Tell you later."

Seeing the promise in her eyes, I continue to help her back to the truck.

"Maddock," Sheree snaps.

That's it! Turning around, I start yelling, "Look, Sheree, I don't give a fuck what you do, but I'm taking Ruby to the truck. We're going to find a hotel, and I'm going to get her warm and look after her. Go for a walk on your own if you need it so badly."

I leave her standing there with her mouth wide open.

We get back to the truck, and I grab the blanket off the back seat. "Take off your pants and wrap yourself in this. I'll find us a hotel."

"Sh-sh-shopping," she stammers.

I roll my eyes as she wraps the towel around her body and shimmies out of her jeans. "Ruby, one day is not going to kill you, but hypothermia might."

I chuck her wet clothes in the back of the truck before easing her into the passenger seat. Sheree has finally reached us, and she huffs at my handling of Ruby and the fact that she has to sit in the back, but I have no fucks left to give. Slamming the door, I run around to the driver's side, not worrying about conjuring another shirt. I just need to get her warm and dry. I pull out my phone and google nearby hotels. The Westin isn't far away, so I start the engine and put it in gear.

I roll down the window. "Either get in or don't, but I'm not waiting for you to have a temper tantrum," I tell Sheree.

She huffs and climbs into the back, slamming the door. I have the truck moving before she has even strapped in.

Arriving at the hotel, I pull into the valet parking, run around to help Ruby out, and then throw my keys at the valet. "No luggage," I tell him, and he nods before climbing in and waiting patiently for Sheree to get out. She's sitting stubbornly inside with her arms crossed, sulking, but I don't care.

I help Ruby into the hotel, and we approach the reception where a woman lifts her head and smiles at us. She is so well trained, she doesn't even blink at my half naked body or Ruby's bedraggled appearance.

I pull out my wallet and hand over my credit card. "Hi, we need a room, one with a bath, please. We've had an accident, and we need to warm her up."

She smiles sympathetically and swipes the card. "Of course, Mr. Crane. How many nights?"

"Just the one for now." She nods and hands me back my card and a key card to a room. "That will be

Room 405. Enjoy your stay, and please don't hesitate to let us know if you need anything."

I thank her and guide Ruby to the elevators. Sheree has come in behind us and now stands between us and the elevators. With her hands on her hips, she demands, "What about me?"

I roll my eyes. "Sheree, when are you going to understand that I don't care?"

She looks like I slapped her, but I feel nothing but disdain for the woman and disgust at myself. What was I doing with her? The woman in my arms is the only one who has ever been on my radar.

Moving around Sheree, I press the button for the elevator. When it arrives, I help Ruby in. She's getting heavy, so I put my arms under her knees and lift her. Her eyes flutter as she struggles to keep them open, but she finally loses the battle. Shit, I need to get her warm. As the elevator door closes, Sheree approaches with a look of fury on her face. A ripple of something crosses her body, but it's too quick for me to know for sure what it is. The door closes, and I wait impatiently for it to reach our floor. When it does, I stride quickly down to our room. Shifting Ruby awkwardly in my arms, I manage to swipe the card and open the door.

I rush inside and lay her on the bed before checking the bathroom. There is a huge tub, but I worry about her staying awake. I really should call a doctor to check on her. Discarding the idea about the bathtub, I run the shower and magically remove my jeans, leaving my boxers on. Moving back to Ruby, I unwrap her from the blanket and leave her just in my shirt and her undies. Another rumble of satisfaction escapes my mouth at seeing her in my shirt. Jesus, caveman much?

Picking her up, I step over to the shower and climb in. The steam engulfs us, and the warm water flows across her body, waking her slightly.

She looks up at me, dazed and confused, but a small smile crosses her face. "Maddock?"

"Yeah, baby," I reply, holding her tightly. She smiles again and rests her head against my chest, sighing in contentment. Looking down, I realize my shirt has molded to her curves and the water has turned it transparent. Although everything is hidden, my cock twitches at the thought and feel of her body pushed against mine. God, the woman almost died. I need to have some patience. I feel slightly guilty, but hey, I am just a man.

We stand here until she stops shaking and can manage to stand on her own. I get out and dry myself, conjuring dry boxers onto my body, and then I hold out a towel for her. She turns off the water and climbs out. I can see the outline of dusky pink nipples through the fabric, and my cock leaps again. Ignoring it, I wrap her in the towel and dry her. She continues to smile at me.

I gesture at her wet clothes, and they disappear

before being replaced by another one of my T-shirts that reaches her knees, but I leave off the underwear. What? Can you blame me? She's still slightly dazed, so I herd her toward the bed, draw back the covers, and help her slide in. Pulling up the quilt, I tuck her in. It's just after lunch, but she needs to recover from her ordeal. Watching her drift off to sleep, I make the decision to reach out to Pru tell her we will stay the night, so I shoot off a text message then tug the blinds shut, set my alarm, and climb in behind her. Body heat is supposed to warm a body, isn't it?

CHAPTER
Fifteen

Ruby

I wake slowly. My throat is sore, like it's been rubbed by sandpaper, and my chest hurts as if a ton of bricks has been sitting on it. My eyelids stick together, but when I manage to open them, I find the room I'm in is dark. I'm lying on my side and there is a hard, hot body wrapped around me, a thick thigh between my legs, and an impressive erection poking me in the backside. I think very carefully about what I had been doing because I might have missed something good, which would make me sad. The memory is just beyond my reach, the fuzziness clearing slowly, but then it all comes back to me and I stiffen in shock. Maddock! Sheree! That bitch pushed me! I wriggle as I try to escape his clutches, but he tightens his hold.

"Ruby, the more you wiggle, the more I like it," a husky voice rumbles in my ear as he nuzzles closer to me, placing little kisses on my neck as he thrusts his cock into my ass.

Goosebumps erupt across my skin, and my nipples pebble into rocks. Oh, my goodness. I stop abruptly. I don't know what to think. Yesterday he felt nothing but loathing for me, and today, well, that's definitely not loathing I feel pushing against me. I mean, I know I shouldn't hold it against him, he was spelled, but I was very hurt.

"I can practically feel your brain working," he murmurs as he rolls off me with a sigh. I instantly miss his delicious warmth and want him to return, but a conversation is needed.

"It was a spell," I whisper quietly. "You were covered in a negativity spell designed to make you indifferent to your friends, family, and especially me," I explain, rolling over to face him. I can't see much in the dark, but the light from under the doorway illuminates the room slightly. He's lying on his back with his hands behind his head.

He huffs out a deep breath. "Yeah, I kind of figured that out after a little bit of soul searching. I thought you removed it the other day."

Sighing, I prop up on one arm, my muscles protesting the movement. "I did! It was redone. I'm not positive, but I'm fairly certain Sheree is some kind of supe. I'm not sure if she's a witch—she just doesn't feel like one—but I think she's masking whatever she is. I will do some more research when we get home."

He puts a hand over his eyes. "My time with her is so foggy, but I remember her wanting to break into Mom's shop for sex," he says, the disgust in his voice evident.

"Yeah, your behavior was definitely not normal. Uhm... I have a confession."

"Mmm? Okay," he replies softly. "It can't be any worse than my behavior has been recently."

"Mom made me do a spell, you drank it in your coffee this morning, and it was supposed to be sealed with a kiss, sneaky bitch that she is, but because you were so anti-me, it didn't happen until you gave me mouth to mouth. That activated it. You are protected now, but we are joined because the spell is bound to me so that I can feel if anyone tries anything." All the details run out of my mouth in a rush.

His head turns toward me, and not being able to see his expression clearly is bothering me, so I sit up and fumble for a lamp. My hand knocks into one on the bedside table, so I find the switch and turn it on. His face is covered in a look of confusion.

"Please don't be angry with me," I beg. "She said it was the only way that would work."

He blows out another deep breath. "Ah, Ruby, I'm

not upset. After how horrible I was to you, I'm surprised you would want to do that." The confusion turns to shame and guilt.

"Maddock," I murmur softly, reaching out to hold his hand. "When will you realize I would do anything for you?"

Heat appears in his eyes, and he reaches out with both hands and pulls me toward him. "I'm going to kiss you now, Ruby. You have to stop me if you don't want it."

Stop him? Not likely! He wraps me up in his arms, holding my head in place and angling it for his pleasure. Our bodies press together, and our legs intertwine. His mouth descends onto mine, and he nips my lips, teasing and tantalizing, before his tongue swipes across my bottom lip, asking for entrance. Melting into him, I sweep my tongue out to taste his, licking and sucking in return. They clash together, wrestling for dominance as we sample each other.

His hands slowly creep up under my shirt, stroking and caressing, lifting it higher and higher. Breaking the kiss, he lifts it over my head before throwing it to the side. His gaze sweeps over my body, and the desire in his eyes and the quirk of his lips tell me he likes what he sees.

"Ruby, I have been imagining you naked in my bed for many years, and let me tell you, it doesn't disappoint," he growls before his head descends and he wraps his lips around one of my nipples, licking and sucking like it's his favorite treat. My eyes roll back in my head and a moan escapes my mouth. Grabbing a handful of his hair, I hold on tight.

Another growl escapes his lips as he swaps breasts, giving my other nipple the same tongue lashing. His hot, wet mouth feels amazing on my skin. My breath hitches as his mouth leaves my breasts and heads south toward my naked pussy. Without delay, he dives in, and another groan escapes my lips as he licks and sucks my folds before moving to my clit. He uses his tongue to circle the tight bundle of nerves, ramping up the fire tingling through my body. Clutching the sheets and biting my lip, I try to keep the noises from falling out of my mouth, but he adds two fingers, thrusting them deep, and I can't stop the exclamation. "God, yes! Fuck, that feels good."

"Oh, Ruby, you're so tight and wet." His thrusts increase in speed, and my hips rise to meet his movements.

I reach down and grind his face into my pussy. He growls his enjoyment.

"Come all over my face, baby." He thrusts hard once more and sucks on my clit. Fireworks explode through my body, and I tip over the edge.

"Oh, God, yes!" I ride it out, my hips still moving with his fingers while his tongue laps lightly, prolonging my orgasm. My body relaxes, and my hands release his hair before I run my fingers through it. He slowly pulls his fingers out and wipes his mouth on my thigh before climbing up my body. His cock nudges against my pussy as he leans down to kiss me lazily, leaving the taste of me in my mouth.

Leaning down, he whispers, "Don't get too relaxed. I'm not done with you yet." Placing a quick kiss on my lips, he rolls off of me and sits up on the bed.

In my dazed, post-orgasmic state, I don't realize what he's doing until I find myself flipped onto my belly with my ass in the air. His calloused hands are rough as he caresses my thighs before working his way up to rub the globes of my ass. Leaning down, he places a gentle kiss on each cheek before taking a bite out of one. A yelp leaves my mouth, and I turn my head to growl at him. He winks at me and playfully slaps my ass.

"Oh, baby, the things I'm going to do to you."

"What makes you think I'm going to let you do more after this?" I ask him. The playful look leaves his eye and he leans forward, and I feel his cock push against my sensitive pussy.

He looks me in the eye. "Don't do that, Ruby, not now. You don't realize how long I've wanted this. You're not getting away now." He kisses me hard and thrusts into me, seating himself fully. He holds still, his cock pulsing inside my tight, wet channel.

We both groan at the sensations, and then with slow thrusts and lazy kisses, he shows me how he feels. He reaches around and runs his calloused hands over my breasts before tweaking my nipples with his fingers. Another groan leaves my mouth. My tingles return, and my orgasm starts to build again. Sitting up, he grabs hold of my hips with a punishing grip and begins to thrust harder and faster. My body bucks against him, our breathing is coming more quickly, and grunts and groans fill the room in a symphony of sex and seduction.

He reaches around, and with a commanding voice, he demands, "Come on my cock, Ruby," as he pinches my clit.

I detonate again. A volcano of desire erupts and flows through my body, and I call out to the heavens. He thrusts a couple more times, pushing through the unyielding grip my pussy has on his cock, before he finishes. His body collapses onto mine, and having no strength left, my sweat-soaked body collapses as well, getting sandwiched between him and the bed. God, his weight feels so good.

He goes to get up, and I shout, "No!" Maddock looks at me quizzically when I turn my head. "Don't go yet, I like it, just wait."

He smiles softly and nuzzles into my neck. The blood pulsing through my veins starts to slow, and our breathing evens out and syncs up. I feel him soften, and he slips out slightly.

Sighing with disappointment, I say, "Okay, roll off, I need to clean up."

He rolls to the side, allowing me to climb off, and I walk gingerly to the bathroom.

"Fuck, my legs." I laugh. "I haven't worked them so hard in a long time."

His eyes darken with desire. "Don't worry, Ruby, you'll be getting plenty of practice."

I laugh at him. "Cocky, aren't you?"

He jumps off the bed and stalks me into the bathroom, trapping me between him and the bench. "No, not cocky, but you're mine now, Ruby. No backsies!" He gives me a cheeky grin with our childhood words and turns, opening the shower and turning on the tap while he whistles a little tune.

A smile slowly crosses my face, and the happiness inside my chest overflows. Hugging myself with joy, I join him in the shower. When I enter, his grin promises me a lot more joy.

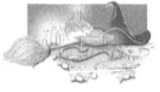

After a soapy, wet, slippery tussle in the shower, we climb out and dry off. Using magic to clothe ourselves, we order some food and settle in for the evening. Room service delivers our food promptly, and we are both sitting on the couch eating when Maddock brings up Morbank Island.

"Why do you think there are so many spells affecting Morbank Island? And what was the point of having one on me?"

Leaning back, I finish chewing my food before answering. "This is just a theory, but I think destabilizing the Arbor Vitae Coven is the main reason. Why they want to do that is anyone's guess," I reply, shrugging my shoulders. "But I would hazard a guess that it has to do with the portal."

He looks thoughtful. "You know, it's funny… Julie was always complaining that she wasn't allowed in the portal room," he muses. "I wonder why she wanted in so badly."

"Of course she wasn't. Only coven and coven descendants are allowed in the room, unless they have off-world blood." I continue to eat, feeling hungry after the eventful day.

"Actually, that's not true, it's just what we tell everyone to keep nosy people away. Regan has even thrown around an idea of off-world tours to the nicer realms as another market to attract visitors to the island."

I look at Maddock in surprise. "Wow, that's actually a great idea. I wonder what the logistics would be and how the realms would feel about that."

Maddock finishes his food and takes a long sip from his beer. "I think Regan has spoken to the shifters, vampires, and elves. None seem opposed to it, but their biggest issue was making them feel like they weren't in a zoo."

Finishing up, I lean back and rub my belly, groaning in contentment. "Let's not worry about Morbank right now. I just want to enjoy this surprise short break. I thought for sure this would be a whirlwind trip and we would be home already." Pulling my legs up on the couch, I snuggle closer to him.

His arm wraps around my shoulders, securing me to his side. "Best surprise ever," he mumbles.

"So much to do tomorrow," I murmur, my eyes drifting closed in contentment.

He laughs and stands up, pulling me with him. Maddock walks me back to the bed, and with a gesture, he magically removes our clothes. "If you're going to fall asleep, let's be comfortable." Laying us down, he pulls me in close and spoons me. His legs tangle with mine, the hairs on them tickling my inner thighs, and I feel his chest rise up and down in a smooth rhythm. His warmth and a feeling of rightness surround me, and I fall asleep with a small smile on my face.

CHAPTER
Sixteen

Ruby

Waking up next to Maddock, whose rugged good looks are illuminated in the little bit of light coming through the curtains, makes this morning the best morning ever. I'm not sure how I'm going to go back to waking up next to a butt licking Sugar. Maybe I need to convince him to have sleepovers.

Sometime during the night, we moved. He is now on his back, and my body is pressed against his, my leg thrown over his waist. I can feel his morning wood pushing against my thigh. Smiling to myself, I climb under the blankets and move down the bed.

Maybe if I wake him up with a blow job he might want to stay over more often. I take his hot, thick cock into my hand and give it a couple of strokes before running my tongue from base to tip. I hear a groan leave Maddock's mouth before he pushes the blankets back and looks down at me with a wicked glint in his eye.

"Best way to wake up ever." His husky voice causes goosebumps to erupt across my skin.

He threads his fingers into my hair, getting a good grip as I take his hardness into my mouth, licking and sucking. His hips make little, tightly controlled thrusts, and his thighs tense in an attempt to not overwhelm me. One of my hands caresses and fondles his balls, tugging on them, while the other joins my mouth on his thick cock.

He grunts and groans with enjoyment, and a musky taste of precum dribbles into my mouth. Maddock pulls me off his cock and drags me up his body, slamming his mouth onto mine. His fingers test the wetness of my pussy before he drives his cock deep inside me, seating himself to the hilt. We groan in unison.

"Best morning ever," I mutter against his mouth.

With our eyes locked and mouths fused, he makes love to me with lazy, languid strokes. When our orgasms peak at the same time, a soul-deep feeling of contentment surrounds me, and I know I'm exactly where I'm meant to be.

After sex, we shower and order some breakfast. When we're ready, we leave the hotel and spend the next few hours running around after supplies. We stack as many twenty-five pound bags of sugar as we can fit in the back of Maddock's truck. I also place an order to be delivered in a few days. I replace all the smashed food colorings and flavors and replace all the different chocolate molds. Luckily Mom ordered all the equipment to be delivered, because the back seat of Maddock's truck is full.

Since we are replacing all the packaging, I sit down with the rep and have a slightly new design made. It's a more modern, fresher design that I hope will attract some new faces. We will add the new logo to the website too.

After getting the last few items on my list and having a quick bite to eat, we start the drive for Morbank Island.

I turn and look at everything on the back seat, commenting, "I wonder what happened to Sheree. Luckily she's not here, there's just no room for her."

He grunts in response. "I'd like to say good riddance, but I have a feeling that's not the last we'll see of her."

I cross to the middle seat and snuggle into him, watching the scenery go by. With a deep breath, I broach another sensitive subject. "I missed you, Maddock. You do realize now that I didn't stay away deliberately, right? I had every intention of only being gone for a couple of months. I just wanted to see some new things before I settled down and ran the store." He keeps his eyes on the road. "I took that conversation we had on my twenty-first birthday very seriously. The kiss that night meant more to me than any other kiss I'd had before, but I had already committed to my trip. I didn't want to be that girl, the one who dropped everything for a boy without seeing what's out there for myself, and you promised you'd wait."

He reaches down and grabs my hand, giving it a squeeze. "When I find out who messed with us, they are going to be very sorry," he growls.

Squeezing his hand in return, I reply, "They are not going to know what hit them. The Arbor Vitae Coven does not like it when you mess with their own."

The rest of the drive home is spent in quiet, peaceful contentment. We catch each other up on our lives and the things we missed while we were apart. Before I know it, he is driving the truck off the ferry and parking in front of the manor guest house. Climbing out with my backpack, I head to the front door and look back at him. When I see he's sitting hesitantly in his truck, a small smile crosses my face.

"Well, are you just going to sit there, or are you going to help me christen my new bed?" I ask, raising my eyebrow, and I laugh when I see him hurry to unbuckle.

He rushes up the path and tackles me, swinging me around and placing kisses all over my neck and face. Giggling like a madwoman, I push him away and open the door to the sunroom. Now that we are home, I use magic to secure his truck overnight. An anti-critter spell will keep away all the bugs, insects, and other nocturnal animals that may be interested in all the bags of sugar sitting in the back of his truck. Grabbing him by the hand, I drag him through the sunroom, unlock the interior door with a wave of my hand, and pull him up the spiral staircase to the loft.

I set the alarm to wake me up early, but luckily Maddock makes my morning interesting again, so when he drops me in front of the store, I have a smile on my face.

I use magic to open up, and the scent of fresh paint hits my nose as I enter, the tinkle of the bell overhead bringing a smile to my face. The shop looks amazing. All the new cabinetry has been installed, and in one corner are the beer barrels I'm going to use for displays. One of the walls is lined with clear, acrylic display boxes, ready to be filled with an assortment of gummy candy, Jelly Bellies, and M&M's. Everything is light and bright, and with the added pop of color, the store will look incredible.

A counter runs the length of one wall with the fudge fridge on one side, the assorted chocolate fridge on the other, and the cash register in the middle. But the pièce de résistance is my candy making area. Directly in the middle of the shop is a large square space blocked off from customers by clear plexiglass. Within the square is my heating and cooling tables, as well as a gas copper kettle boiler. They must have arrived earlier than Mom thought. There are some storage cabinets for flavors and colorings and the different tools we'll need. There is also a candy puller, batch roller, and wrap and cut machines for the taffy we plan to make. Everything looks shiny and new.

Excitement floods my veins as the doorbell rings again, announcing Maddock's arrival. In his arms is a bag of sugar. Rushing toward him, I hold the door open so he can maneuver the big bag inside.

"The old kitchen is now a storage area. Just put it out there, and I'll magic the rest inside." He heads toward the storage room as I peer out the door. "Are there many people outside?" I ask before it closes, but the street looks deserted this early in the morning, and a fine mist from the river still coats the ground. "I'm going to make all the hard candy and taffy today, so that should keep me busy until the rest of the supplies arrive," I tell him, still peering through the window.

I feel a pair of hands on my hips, and his warm breath blows across my neck as he nuzzles close. A smile crosses my face as I lean back into his broad body, feeling relaxed and content for the first time in forever.

"I need to get going. Jandar is bringing a couple more horses over to have their feet done," he mutters distractedly while placing kisses on my neck. "Do you want to come to my place tonight?"

"You have a house?" I ask, turning to him in surprise. A smile crosses his face as he pulls me in close, almost nose to nose.

"Yes, Ruby. I'm an adult, I have my own place now. Did you think I was inviting you to stay at Mom and Dad's?" He laughs.

Blushing, I shake my head in embarrassment. "No, I'm just still realizing how much has changed since I've been gone."

He places a gentle kiss on my lips. "Let me know when you are done. I'll come and get you." He opens the door and walks out to the truck.

Waving my hand, I magic the rest of the supplies into the storeroom out the back.

After watching him drive down the street to his workshop, I head back to the storeroom. In here, I have an enrober for covering things with chocolate and plenty of drying area for the cream centers for the specialized chocolates, and a small room to the side is designed explicitly for making starch molds for the cream centers. There is also plenty of storage for boxes, wrapping, and all the other bits and pieces involved in making candy.

A thrill runs through my veins as I start planning today's jobs. Writing on the whiteboard Bram hung for me, I make a list of taffy. We might as well get the easy stuff done first since I don't need help with that, as opposed to some of the other treats. I make a note to call Jenna and let her know I need her, but I plan on putting it off as long as possible. Deciding to start with my favorite, I pull out the apple pie flavoring and the green and brown colors. Whistling, I gesture and magic my Bluetooth speaker from home to the store. Pulling my phone out of my pocket, I load up an old-school Britney playlist and start measuring the sugar, glucose, and water.

Using magic and my candy making talents, I make three batches of taffy before Mom and Dad arrive around midmorning. The bell above the door tinkles, announcing their arrival, but I had already seen them through the front window of the store. It is awesome having the candy making area out front.

"Hi," I mumble around a mouthful of taffy. Hey, it's quality control. "What are you guys doing here?"

"We just got a call that the barge with the deliveries has arrived, so we thought we would come in and give you a hand. If we unpack, then you won't have to stop."

A warm feeling fills my heart. Thank God for family. "You guys rock," I tell them, smacking kisses on both their cheeks.

"We're just so happy you are home," Dad replies, patting my hand and heading outside to the truck that pulled up at the curb.

I turn to Mom and find her studying me carefully.

"The spell worked, I can tell."

Blushing again, I arch an eyebrow at her. "You can, can you?"

She just pats my cheek before she follows Dad outside. "Your shirt is buttoned wrong. I'm happy for you, Ruby. I knew it would work out." Her smug tone floats back to me over her shoulder.

Looking down, I realize she's right. Shaking my head, I shrug it off, the memory of this morning canceling out any embarrassment I feel at my mother's knowing look.

The next two weeks fly by, and by the time the weekend comes around, I'm exhausted. I worked late every night and fell into bed next to Maddock, either at his or my place, and promptly drifted off to sleep. I haven't seen Regan or the children for days, and I'm suffering from withdrawals, but he's been just as busy as me.

But that's going to change today. Regan is bringing the children into town to see the new store, and we are going to grab some ice cream. I'm hoping Maddock will join us as well. Regan knows the spell worked, but Maddock and I wanted to get used to the idea of an *us* before we shared it around, so this will be our first venture out in public together. I am as giddy as a schoolgirl.

My store will be ready to go Monday. I had supes distribute flyers in the realms, advertising the special spelled candy I made and set up at home. I've also been posting on social media and sending out flyers to everyone I can think of, telling them about the special spelled candy for humans. Our grand opening is going to be on Monday, so I am going to take the next day and a half easy, because who knows when I will get some downtime next. The special orders have started to roll in again also, so Jenna and I will be kept busy.

Regan, Kady, and Kadir arrive first. The kids' excited giggling reaches my ears even before the doorbell does. Leaving the storeroom where I was doing inventory, I head out front. Before I can get very far, I'm attacked by two very exuberant children.

"Aunt Wuby, we missed you," Kadir says, burying his face against my leg and squeezing hard.

Not to be outdone, Kady grabs the other leg. "Aunt Ruby, can you please take Jenna? She's not very nice."

Regan smothers a laugh. "No, Kady, that's not very nice."

The kids pull away, not apologetic at all. The look of awe covering their faces as they take in the shop renovations is enough to bring a proud smile to my face.

"Holy cannoli, this is awesome!" Kadir yells, jumping up and down.

Kady tugs on my hand, and with a pleading look, she asks, "Can we have some? Please?" Her wide-eyed look of innocence is not fooling me.

Crossing my arms, I question, "What did Dad say?"

A frown crosses both their faces. "He said we were having ice cream and couldn't have any." Kady confesses.

I look at Regan, and he winks at me. "Well, I can't really go against your dad," I say, going over to the taffy tubs and grabbing two of the small serving bags. "But if you fill these with taffy, I'm sure you can take them home and eat them later." The pure joy and happiness on their faces remind me exactly why I love making candy. They go to grab the bags, but I hold them out of their reach. "What do we need to do?"

"Always clean our teeth after eating candy," they chorus together. I hand them their bags, and they run to fill them as the doorbell rings and Maddock walks in. Regan observes warily as Maddock walks straight past him, pulls me into his body, and lays a sweet but sexy kiss on my lips.

"Hi, beautiful. I missed you."

The sound of cheering behind me breaks into our bubble, and we turn to see the kids and Regan all clapping their hands.

"About time," Regan remarks as he wraps his arms around us. "I'm so happy for you. It's about time something went right around here. Hopefully this is just the start."

Epilogue

Ruby

Pulling the rental car to a stop, I engage the parking brake and blow out a massive breath of air. The grand opening of the shop was a huge success, and we sold out of the spelled human candy within hours, but it wasn't enough to keep the tourists hanging around. We really need to revitalize the rest of the businesses in the hope they will come to town and stay a few days to explore all it has to offer. Regan has his realm tours in hand, but it's time to start nudging the rest of the Tempting Ten in the right direction.

As I stare at the little gelato shop in front of me, and the warm, Amalfi Coast breeze drifts through the open window, I think about how hard this may be. Stepping out of the car, I push my sunglasses on top of my head and lean over to grab the potion out of the drink holder. Mom and I decided a dose of the same potion we gave Maddock would do the trick, but this time I didn't use my blood to anchor it, I used Regan's. I don't think he caught on to what I was doing when I *accidentally* stabbed him at dinner at Mom and Dad's. The portal fluctuations were running him ragged, and he was dealing with some irate supes who were unable to get in and out as needed. These fluctuations were what made me decide to come. It has never happened before.

Maddock stayed behind. His mom is busy now that Sheree is no longer working for her, and Melody is only able to work weekends. Luckily the weather is cooling, so the ice cream store isn't too busy, but he stayed to support her anyway. He's also helping Regan with his plans, and there is a critical commission he's working on. I couldn't really spare the time either, but with Dad's retirement on hold for a little longer and Jenna's help, they will manage for a couple of days.

Through the window, I see the familiar dark head of my best friend. Tatiana has been dodging my calls, or maybe all the way over here in Italy she was unaffected by the spell cast by the coven. Whatever the reason, I decided enough was enough. Pushing through the door, I wait patiently for her to finish serving the customers, and when she finally slows down, I approach the counter.

"Bitch, you better not have been ghosting me." A look of shock crosses her face as her head swings in my direction. A beautiful smile curves her lips as she races around the counter and throws her arms around me.

"Ruby!" she exclaims, hugging me hard. "What are you doing here?" Her blue eyes shine with tears as she holds me at arm's length.

"Did you think after all the times I called and messaged and you didn't respond that I wouldn't be hunting you down?"

A frown crosses her face and her fingers tighten briefly on my arm before she pulls them back, crossing her arms defensively. "I did no such thing. I wouldn't ever ignore you. I haven't heard from you in months."

Looking at her face, I decide the spell or some unseen force must be at work, because her aura says she's telling the truth. "Well, there are some things I need to tell you. Can we grab a coffee?"

Nodding, she says, "Just let me tell the owner I'm grabbing some lunch."

I watch her step behind the counter and back to what I assume is the kitchen. Before long, she returns, and we head to a coffee shop for a long story that I hope won't upset her too much.

An hour or so later, we are sitting in my car, driving to her apartment. Tear tracks still stain her face from when I told my story.

"I still can't believe it," she says, shaking her head. "I would never leave Mom like that. I need to tell Marco that I have to head home for a couple of weeks. I'm not sure if he will be able to get away. He works such long hours for his father's law firm, always in late and early meetings. I don't see him very often at the moment. Hopefully he won't be too mad."

I park in an available space, and we get out and head to a block of fancy apartments.

"Wow," I murmur, looking around. "These are really lovely." I smile at the doorman as we walk to the elevators.

She smiles. "Marco's parents own it and let us stay here." We enter the elevator, and she pushes the button for the top floor. "So what kind of backlash did your mom say might happen from the spell she and the older ladies cast?"

"All sorts of doom and gloom apparently. Mom thinks that Mr. Whitmore's heart attack was due to the spell." I pull the potion out of my handbag. I didn't want anyone to give us strange looks at the coffee shop, so I didn't give it to her earlier. "Here, you need to drink this in case the spell didn't reach here."

She takes it and downs it by the time the doors open to the penthouse. I watch as a wave of my magic flows over her body. She instantly stands taller and looks less burdened. "Wow, I feel so much lighter, and everything is clearer."

I nod my head as we both step out but stop dead at the sound we hear. "Um, Tats, either you left the porn channel on, or I think we may be seeing one of those backlash issues now."

A look of fury crosses her face, and she storms toward the back of the penthouse where I now hear yelling and screaming. I wince at the flurry of Italian that flows out of Tatiana's mouth. I don't know much, but I'm pretty sure her words are not for polite company. A naked blonde comes running from that direction with clothes clutched in her hand. She steps around me and frantically presses the button for the elevator.

Tatiana follows her out.

"I'm not sure about backlash. This may just be a case of an asshole," she says, flinging a high heel shoe in the woman's direction. A determined expression crosses her face. "Book the tickets, Ruby. Nothing is keeping me here now. Morbank Island, watch out, I'm coming home."

Afterword

Thank you for reading!
I hope you enjoyed the book. It would be super awesome if you could leave a review, because I'd love to hear what you thought of the story

Are you ready for Tatiana's story?
Available soon on Amazon

.

Acknowledgments

Thank you to Tash from Dazed Designs for my cover.
I love it so much.

Thank you to Jess from Elemental editing who
helped make things all tidy for me.

Thank you to all the readers who took a chance and
picked up this book. I can't begin to tell you how
much it means to me.

Coming Soon

<u>*Dreamy Delights*</u>
Arbor Vitae Coven 2

Prologue

"This meeting of the Matrons of Morbank Island may come to order," Prudence Miller announces as she bangs her gavel on the lectern in front of her. The excited chatter of the ladies dulls more quickly than usual, but they have so many things to discuss and not much time.

"As I'm sure you all know by now, the spell worked," she announces, but she shakes her head somewhat ruefully. "Sort of! My Ruby has returned."

The ladies surrounding her burst into applause, some a little less enthusiastically than others, but that's to be expected. Pru sweeps a sympathetic look around the room.

"I know it's not the outcome we expected, but it's a start. There are some very dark forces working against us, but never fear, ladies, we will overcome these obstacles, and I have no doubt that we will prevail."

This time the round of applause is more enthusiastic.

"As me meet, Ruby is on a plane to Italy to drag Tatiana home. We think it is possible some of them are just too far away to be affected by the spell, so she is armed with the same anti-negativity potion that we used on Maddock."

Looking around the room, she casts a spell to ensure privacy. "We have anchored Tatiana's potion to Regan. I know," she says, holding her hands up. "I can see your skeptical looks. Ruby and I decided if we anchored the potion to someone in town who is unaffected that we would have a better chance of overcoming it. It's just a light anchor, and no one's forcing anyone together or anything, although I know that I, for one, wouldn't mind more grandbabies and Lucille and Phillip feel the same way," she explains, her lips stretching into a cheeky smile.

Lucille nods her head enthusiastically. "I am praying to the goddess that Ruby is successful. I'm so grateful Maddock is sorted out and we got rid of Sheree. I love having Melly work for me, but I'm ready to retire. I want to start enjoying life a little more. I'd rather ask for forgiveness than permission," she states stubbornly, crossing her arms.

"One by one we will drag those girls home, kicking and screaming if need be, but I'm sure it won't come to that. I'm also thinking we'll need to perform the same spell we did before on the full moon, adding in each returned girl's power. By the next full moon, hopefully both Ruby and Tatiana will be able to add their power to it."

Everyone shows their agreement with head nods, murmuring, "Yes."

"So that is the daughter situation update. Now, on to another pressing problem—the portal. Over the last few weeks we have had a few issues. The portal has faded briefly three times. Luckily no one was attempting to realm travel when this happened, but we've had to limit travel to twice a week until we can get it fixed. Tuesdays and Fridays will be travel times. In short, we need an influx of tourists. Regan has scheduled more meetings with the heads of the fae, vampire, and shifter realms to finalize his realm tour programs. They have been approved, so now it is just a matter of working out the nitty-gritty details."

"I don't understand this at all," Fiona Blackwood says, shaking her head. "We have had periods of low tourism before. Let's face it, a hundred years ago we didn't have any tourists at all, and the portal still functioned perfectly. There must be something else that is interfering with the portal's power."

"What about on the realm side of the portal?" Minerva Crowe asks. "Maybe we need to send someone in to investigate that side."

Pru purses her lips before nodding her head. "Yes, but we need to be diplomatic about it. We can't accuse anyone or point fingers, or they will get upset."

"What about asking Regan to keep an eye out for things when he goes for his final meetings?" Beatrix adds.

"What about the mayor? He's a vampire, so maybe he can put some feelers out?" Denise Shelly suggests. "He's so kind, I'm sure he would like to help if we explain the situation."

Prudence's heart sinks. She was hoping to keep it a secret for now, but the coven does have a responsibility to the town and the other supernaturals living in it.

"You're all right. It's time to share this and get some more heads and hearts working on the problem. I wouldn't want the paranormal council to accuse us of not doing everything we can."

"So we decided to come to you for help. It's become a whole town issue now, not just the coven's. Someone is out to destroy us. The candy store was vandalized a few weeks ago, as well as Ruby's car. Things are starting to escalate," Pru says, updating Mayor Lucas Sharpe on the issues surrounding the island, the coven, and the portal.

Sitting behind a wide, wooden desk, Mayor Sharpe wears a stylish gray suit that makes his eyes look even grayer than normal.

The frown on his face grew increasingly deeper as the story progressed. Blowing out a deep breath as she finishes, he sits back in his chair with an expression of exasperation crossing his features as he processes the information. "You should have come to me sooner, Pru. I know I haven't been mayor of this town for very long, and that I'm still a stranger compared to the founding families of the island, but I care and I want to be able to help the community any way I can."

She wiggles under his stern gaze but straightens her back and replies, "Yes, I know, but we all make mistakes. Trust is a little thin on the ground at the moment, but I will endeavor to do better," she promises, looking a little embarrassed.

"Well, pointing the finger of blame is not going to help the situation now, Mayor Sharpe. At least Mom realized her error and has now fixed it. Let's move on, shall we?" Regan suggests, breaking the tension in the room.

The mayor nods. "Yes, of course, and call me Lucas. It sounds like you already have some plans in the works. I'll put out some feelers of my own, but let's work on a few more things to bring the tourists back."

Both Pru and Regan nod their heads.

Regan speaks up. "Well, I have my realm tourism plans in the works, and we are just waiting on a few more approvals. I was thinking that while we are waiting for that, maybe the manor could run a haunted house for Halloween this year and sell tickets. Also, with coven help, we could turn the open grassy space into a cornfield and run a maze as well. We could have hayrides through the orchards and apple picking, and maybe an apple cider stand and pumpkin carving. We could even bring in a band and make it a real town event."

The look on Pru's face changes from worried to enthusiastic. "Regan, that's a fantastic idea. What do you think, Mayor?"

He has a thoughtful expression on his face. "That's a great start. How about the coven starts working on that, Pru? Regan, you concentrate on the tours, because I think that will be very popular. I have an idea about the band, so leave that to me."

Pru and Regan nod.

"Also, let's keep the momentum going. I was

thinking we can have a town Thanksgiving celebration in the town square. Maybe a feast?"

Pru is practically bouncing on her chair in excitement. "Oh, and some fireworks! We can call it Feast and Fireworks, and sell turkey legs and pie and maybe have some old-fashioned games and dress up in period pieces. What a great idea!"

Regan stands, and Lucas and Pru follow suit.

"Okay, so we have some ideas. Let's keep in contact, schedule a few meetings, and get this town revitalized. Once we get the portal issue fixed, we can deal with whoever is behind the spells." A grave look crosses the mayor's face. "When I find out who has messed with my town, they will be sorry."

Pru shudders at the violence in his tone. Up until now, one could forget that the mayor is a vampire, but after the cold, callous way he just said that, she wouldn't want to be in the shoes of the person responsible.

Buy it now DREAMY DELIGHTS